ethereal

Celestra Series
Book 1

ADDISON MOORE

Edited by: Sarah Freese

Cover & Interior Design by: Gaffey Media

Books by Addison Moore:

New Adult Romance

Someone to Love (Someone to Love 1)
Someone Like You (Someone to Love 2)
Someone For Me (Someone to Love 3)
3:AM Kisses (3:AM Kisses 1)
Winter Kisses (3:AM Kisses 2)
Sugar Kisses (3:AM Kisses 3)
Whiskey Kisses (3:AM Kisses 4)
Beautiful Oblivion
The Solitude of Passion
Perfect Love (A Celestra Novella)
Celestra Forever After

Young Adult Romance

Ethereal (Celestra Series Book 1)
Tremble (Celestra Series Book 2)
Burn (Celestra Series Book 3)
Wicked (Celestra Series Book 4)
Vex (Celestra Series Book 5)
Expel (Celestra Series Book 6)
Toxic Part One (Celestra Series Book 7)
Toxic Part Two (Celestra Series Book 7.5)
Elysian (Celestra Series Book 8)
Ephemeral (The Countenance Trilogy 1)

Evanescent (The Countenance Trilogy 2)
Entropy (The Countenance Trilogy 3)
Ethereal Knights (Celestra Knights)

For the mafia princess and the backseat boys.
You mean everything to me.

Preface

Falling in love is a lot like death. It chooses you. It decides the moment and the chain of events that will preclude the precise intersection of life in which it occurs. It uses you—treats you as though you were malleable in its warm pliable hands. It doesn't bother to ask if you want it, or need it, just fills the gaping hole of destiny's design.

Love. My world blooms with its beautiful never-ending ache. I would give all of my blood to my enemies to have it completely—if I knew it would satisfy them—if I could live without it. But I know the resolution. I know the end of the story before it ever begins. I must choose love. And for this, I will surely die.

It is that time in my life—a time for love and a time for death. Fate had intertwined the two, bereaved of any mercy. It is in the architecture of my being, the infrastructure. The pillars of my life had been established long ago—the blueprint written in my bloodlines.

1

Move

A white stagnant cloud surrounds us—fog so thick it makes the world look ethereal—like a relic from some long forgotten place. Our car glides off the ferry, and my stepfather takes the keys from the porter.

Tad, my stepfather, hands him a crumpled bill in secret. Tad is the cheapest living creature on the face of the earth. I'm embarrassed to look at the porter so I begin with the business of climbing in the car.

"Skyla," my mother pulls me back, "let your sisters go first."

My sister Mia, and stepsister Melissa, both crawl into the third row of the minivan. I'm stuck with Drake, per usual, my half brother who entertains himself with bodily functions and tries to get me in on the action. He'll be a junior next month like me.

My mother thought it was a sign that she and her then boyfriend had kids the same ages, plus two deceased spouses. I'm really happy for Mia since both she and Melissa are going into seventh grade together. Junior high in general is kind of scary, plus she's off my back now. Before Melissa came into our lives, Mia was constantly bugging me and getting into my things, and now it's like I don't even exist. Drake on the other hand, I'm not so thankful for. I'm already aware that his presence will effortlessly degrade my social standing.

I push in my ear-buds and lean back for the ride.

Paragon Island is off the central coast of Washington. My mother made a list of odd facts about it and stuck it to the vanity just above my desk, which isn't there anymore because everything I own has been shipped to our new residence somewhere on the west side of the island. I don't remember the laundry list of ridiculous facts, just that it's twenty-six miles in length, two high schools, two malls, and is complete with a load of freaks that specialize in the art of inbreeding. And by the use of deductive logic, some of those freaks will be my classmates— inmates—for the next two years. OK, that last one wasn't actually on the list, but factual nonetheless. Also, there's the whole deal about east side, west side, which suggests to me I should be expecting musical gang fights and lots of girls named Maria.

I already miss my old school—old life. Not that I was super popular or anything, but it was home and what I was used to. No one had any real expectations of me, and I was comfortable in my nonexistent clique of girls. I also miss my dad who died two years ago, whose death is the entire reason my universe disbanded. He was the gravity that kept my sanity aligned. Without him I'm adrift in this world, without a compass and without a home.

I wipe a lone tear off my face and force myself to take in the landscape—row after row of skeletal trees that stretch to the sky, fog-laden roads illuminated in black and white. Something about this feels right. This is how I imagined the world right after my dad died—lonely—one solid grey scene after the next in some muted old-time movie. L.A. was always sunny, always telling the wrong story, ending with miraculous sunsets that looked like they belonged in a fairytale. It was a murky grey reality that I craved. It's like this island knows me. It knows me right through to my gossamer riddled heart.

"Is it always like this?" I pluck out an ear-bud and lean toward Mom.

"The weather? Rains a lot, too." She beams her paper white teeth in my direction, her crimson hair fringes her face. She knows how to radiate a smile, how to pull one off even when the situation doesn't warrant it. I wish she could turn down the volume once in a while, but that would be like asking the sun to tone down its beams. Sometimes I hate how perky she is, like she doesn't miss dad—like he never existed.

"Perfect." I move my lips, don't let my voice escape.

Tad points toward a long stretch of homes. These aren't the run of the mill suburban streets that stamped out Los Angeles like a disorganized quilt. These houses sit on top of long narrow driveways, each on their own perch, nestled in a private forest of pine trees so thick you can hardly make out the structure of the home itself.

"Third one," Tad says, hovering over the steering wheel.

Now would be a great time for the airbag to deploy. I imagine his shocked expression as it explodes into his chest, knocks him backward and breaks his neck. I can practically see the blood trickle from his nose.

"We're here," my mother sings.

My mouth drops open as we trail up the driveway. It looks massive compared to the beach bungalow we lived in back home. A wall of glass looks out at the street below, tall double doors with twin fixed windows set in both—one of them broken. It takes a minute for me to absorb the sheer mammoth size before I realize it's nothing more than an overgrown cabin. Large fat beams run across the façade, and it reminds me of the Lincoln logs I used to play with in preschool.

The fresh damp air hits me as I file out of the car, baptizes me with the unexpected scent of eucalyptus. I like it like this— nature all around—perfumed air to greet each day. I think I could get used to living here. Paragon is proving to be morbidly beautiful in its own special way.

Drake emerges from the car picking at his nose, his eyes glued to the house in a daze.

Suffice it to say, I'm more than slightly mortified to be forcibly associated with him. Drake is my own personal social suicide, and the sooner I accept that, the sooner I can come to terms with my loner status at the school library.

"Landon family?" A light female voice calls out from the fog at the bottom of the driveway.

A thin brunette with her hair pulled back wafts in and out of the fog like a ghost. Auburn highlights electrify her ponytail as she jogs up to meet us.

"Hi! I'm your neighbor," she jerks her thumb at the house next door, "Brielle." Her tiny hand jets out in my direction.

I reach for her, but Drake sideswipes me. He over exaggerates a handshake, lets her know he's a douchebag right from the beginning. No sense in saving the surprise for later.

"Skyla Messenger." I shove Drake aside with my shoulder and shake her hand like a human who actively participates in civilization.

She reminds me of the army of Barbie's I used to play with as a kid, same perfect features—bright green eyes. Except for the hair. I've got the requisite blonde hair that you need to survive in L.A. If you're a female and have access to a bottle of bleach you're required to go bimbo by the time your sixteen. Lucky for me it grows out of my head this way. I let it grow long after my dad died. It's him I get the curls from.

"Come on." Tad waves us up the stairs onto an expansive porch and the wood groans from the weight of us. A picnic table sits abandoned in the corner with an umbrella is spiked through the center, chock full of spider webs.

"I'll give you the tour," Brielle offers, stepping in before me. She bounces through the door with far more enthusiasm than I've had in years.

Tad and Mom head toward the back of the house, with my mother pointing out how nice everything is and Tad refuting her claims. The girls take off upstairs and fill the hollowed out house with the echoes of their laughter.

"You've been here?"

"Oh yeah, tons. My friend used to live here." Her face smoothes out as she stares past me with a glazed look in her eye.

"Where'd she go?"

"She died."

I stop abruptly, stunned by the revelation. I don't know why I wasn't expecting death as an answer. Sometimes it feels as if death is something unique to my family. I keep forgetting its necrotic arms stretch out to the rest of the world as well.

"You didn't know?" Brielle takes me by the hand and pulls me up the stairs at a decent clip—her enthusiasm still awkwardly bubbling to the surface.

"No. So, um, what happened?" Truth is, I don't want to know. I hate ghost stories by the campfire, and I don't listen to the news. I can't stand freaky things so I avoid them at all costs, that's exactly why I maintain the ability to sleep at night. But this is different. The poor girl lived here once. I should at least care to ask what happened, but Brielle doesn't say anything just keeps walking with a hop in her step as though she didn't hear.

We make our way down a huge hallway with coffee stained walls—cobwebs in the corner, dense enough to qualify as curtains. I watch as the ghostlike tendrils of spider webs long forgotten give a gentle wave from the crevices of the dusty chandelier above.

Mia and Melissa have staked their claim to the bedroom at the far end, near a set of double doors, which I assume is the master. Drake is already gassing up the one just off the stairs, so I'm left with the one in the middle.

"Chloe's room," the words whisper from her lips. Brielle steps in and drinks it down, wide-eyed and terrified.

"Chloe's room," I echo. An icy chill penetrates my bones. I look around at the dingy rectangle with bare walls and dark-planked floors. A large bay window with a built in bench fills the back wall. It lends the room a romantic appeal in a haunted sort of way.

"So your friend—" I start in slow. The last things I want is to do is pull the pin on the grieving grenade in the event it's still fresh—in case her death still stings like hell to think about like it does with my dad. "What did she die of?"

Brielle's face bleeds out all color, her eyes widen at my seemingly irresponsible oversight.

"She didn't die of anything. She was murdered."

2

Adulation

It doesn't take long before I talk my way out of unpacking duties and ditch the haunted house for a quick tour of Paragon Island piloted by Brielle herself.

The movers pull in just as we leave and I see them haul my old dresser out and hoist it upstairs. It looks so foreign here against the backdrop of the pines. All of my furniture, all of my things transplanted to this unknowable place. It scares me on some level knowing life will never be the same again.

"They never caught who did it," Brielle says as we drive down a black velvet highway. "Found her in a shallow grave near the base of Devil's Peak. It's weird because we hang out at the overlook all the time." She pulls her leg up on the seat and steers the wheel with her knee for a good stretch of road. "And there she was right there at the bottom." Her eyes glaze over as tears begin to fall.

I'm too busy honing in on her sorrow, matching it with my own over my father to notice we've drifted lanes. A horn blares without ceasing and shakes us both back to reality. I grab a hold of the wheel and help maneuver us into the proper lane.

"Crap!" I'm half laughing. It feels good like this to have the laughter chase the tears away. One more solid second, and we would have flooded the Jeep with a river of sorrow.

"I'm so freaking sorry," she says, pressing her hand to her chest. "Trust me vehicular homicide wasn't high on my to-do list when I got up this morning." She lifts a finger over at the bowling alley across the way. "Let's go there."

Paragon Bowling Alley, the large neon sign blinks with all the fanfare of some D list joint off the Sunset Strip. It sits across the main thoroughfare, overlooking a jagged shoreline. The sun's dismal glow illuminates it from behind a mass of dark clouds. It sets over the establishment like an orange ember as if prophesying something about that very place.

We make our way inside and a violent seizure of light attacks our senses, subtle as a funhouse. The name *Arcade Heaven* is painted on a plank right above the doorway. The dark cloistered room is lined with video games that blink on an off in a spastic stream of energy. A group of teenagers, mostly Goth looking guys, hunch over the blinking mechanisms making hasty strides with every jerk of their hand.

"This way!" Her voice rises up over the noise.

She leads me through the tiny room and into a well-lit expanse devoid of the sensory pollution of the entry. It looks like your average bowling alley with lanes lining the two opposing walls of the colossal structure. A giant squared off cashier's station sits to our right with a wall of shoes behind it. Every now and again a set of pins knock over followed by a gasp or scream. The place is nearly empty, but then it is a Thursday afternoon in August. I suppose even the village shut-ins take a vacation now and again.

"Bree," a male voice spikes from behind.

We turn in unison. A pair of guys around our age make their way over, both tall, one with gold hair that matches my own, and one with hair the color pitch. It's the blonde that gets my attention. He looks familiar and yet I can't place why. He presses out a smile and my insides explode with heat. It feels as though the entire room has lost its light, harnessed all the beauty life has to offer and shifted its lust-filled focus on the two of us. I bask in his perfection, straight Roman nose, sharp almond eyes, broad chest, shoulders as wide as a baseball bat.

My mouth falls open stupidly, and I can feel the drool pooling beneath my tongue.

"Guys, this is Skyla. She's moving into Chloe's old house." She gives an apprehensive look. "Skyla, these are the knuckleheads I work with, Logan and Gage." She waves her hands over them as though they were prizes.

Logan.

Immediately I'm lost in his trance—like he's cast a spell on me and now I can't look away. It's simultaneously the most comfortable and frightening feeling in the world. I want to tell him that he's gorgeous, that he could start a forest fire with his looks alone, but something far more banal escapes my lips in the form of hello.

"Skyla?" The dark haired boy leans in. "Gage Oliver." He takes up my hand and steps into me in an effort to capture my attention. He smiles and his face ignites in a set of severe dimples that make me weak at the knees. His eyes are the purest color blue I have ever seen—the color of a cobalt sea off in some exotic part of the world. His stunning features are a work of art, and I'm perplexed that standing before me are two of the best looking guys on the planet. Normally, I would have been ripe to worship at his feet, but it's the Adonis to his left that has me spellbound.

"You have a very unique name. It's beautiful." The Adonis takes my hand away from Gage and brings it to his lips with a smile. "*Logan* Oliver." His voice dips as he emphasizes his first name.

"Oh, so you're brothers?" It comes out doubtful. They look nothing alike. Or maybe they're step? Mothers marrying morons *is* on the rise.

"Cousins." Logan ticks his head toward Gage. "I live with them. My parents are both deceased."

His words jar me from my lust-struck stupor.

"Oh, I'm sorry. My dad died, too." It's only when I look down that I notice he's still holding my hand, cradling it soft between both of his. The awkwardness of the situation comes to light and he gently replaces it next to my waist.

"Sorry." He gives a pensive stare, bearing right through me with those amber lenses—like he sees me, but too much. I feel naked under his watchful supervision, and it sends an errant shudder up my spine.

We reconfigure at a nearby table with Brielle next to me, and Logan across from her.

"So you're a junior?" Gage rasps his knuckles across the table like a nervous habit. He's fixed on me with those piercing blue orbs, pulling his gaze across my features slow as honey. He takes me in with an open intensity as if he sees our future written across my forehead.

"Yup," I try to sound casual, ignoring the fact I'm shaking in their godlike presence. "And you guys?"

"We're *all* juniors!" Brielle rattles my arm as though it were the most exciting news in the world.

When she touches my flesh, I can hear her thoughts. It's an odd gift that I underutilize. I think my mother is onto me because she bolts like a cat out of water if I dare let a hug linger.

Bet they're both already in love with her. She glances at the ceiling. *All that perfect hair, and what color are those eyes anyway? Crystal clear? Really, I hate how beautiful she is.*

She hates my beauty. The thought of it brings a slight curve to my lips.

"So tell me about Chloe," I ask no one in particular. If I'm going to be holed up in her bedroom, it'd be nice to know something about her.

A stunted silence fills the tiny space around us, and I suddenly get the feeling I should never have brought her up.

Logan's face darkens. His eyes flare, something akin to anger. Gage cuts a look across the room as though he were seething.

Chloe may be dead, but it's clear her name still holds a great deal of power.

3

Cult of Personality

Turns out Chloe was the subject of much lust at West Paragon High—cheerleader, all around American girl, dated both Logan and Gage on and off—been dead a good nine months.

I blink up at the canopy above my bed. My mother had the movers replicate my old bedroom under her strict delegation of authority. She dreams of us falling in love with this rat-trap, playing the piano and singing by a roaring fire. I think she needs an entire family transplant for something of that moronic magnitude to happen. Doesn't she realize our family died two years ago? We buried it back in L.A. with my father.

I glance out the window as the morning stretches out in a sheer bloom of fog, and a sad smile plays on my lips. Already I don't want to leave—already I'm in love with this haunted, arid island.

I dreamed of Logan last night. Logan on the beach, Logan at the movies, his oven-hot hands racing up and down my body— crying out my name on a lonely stretch of highway.

A horn goes off outside in a series of short staccato beeps.

I glance over at the alarm—nine on the button. Brielle managed to convince me to join the cheerleading squad with her. She said, ever since Chloe died they've yet to fill the void and wouldn't take no for an answer.

The horn goes off again as I round my legs over the bed. I ignore her impatient honking and head into the shower.

When I get out, I find Brielle is sitting Indian style on my bed, messing with her phone. "Morning sunshine." She doesn't bother looking up.

"So Gage or Logan, which one's yours?" I try to sound indifferent, lacing my words with sarcasm, but I'm digging for the truth and we both know it.

I towel dry my hair like it's no big deal, like I didn't whisper I love you to him all night long in my dreams.

"Which one do you think?" She cocks her head to the side like a dare.

It couldn't be Logan. What we shared was electric.

"Gage?"

She pulls her lips in a line. "Neither."

"Oh." I let my towel fall to the ground and snatch the hairbrush off my desk. "Which one are you hoping for?" I can spot a crush a mile away. If she says neither I'm going to hold her down by the wrists until I hear the truth stream through her mind.

"I don't know. I've known them all my life—kind of find them boring. I like fresh meat. You know, undiscovered terrain." She gives a hard squint and points toward Drake's room.

"Oh, dear God, no." In a way it's a good thing because there won't be any weirdness between us, like *ever*. Let the record show I will never challenge her for Drake's affection.

"What?" She breaks out in a giant grin. "He's cute."

"Gah!" My hands rise instinctively over my ears. "It's like you're cursing."

"Anyway," she tosses her phone onto the mattress, "they're not seeing anybody. And when I went to work last night it was obvious they were already warring over you. Guess they like fresh meat, too."

Warring?

My entire body flushes with heat.

Fresh meat, indeed. Good thing I'm partial to carnivores.

West Paragon High sits landlocked an unfortunate distance from the miles of sandy shore the island has to offer. Another fog filled afternoon greets us, and I welcome the dew as it kisses my face, caresses my arms and legs as we cut through it with haste.

We're a good forty minutes late to practice because of my 'hygiene habit' as Brielle so delicately put it.

On the ride over, she informed me of the *triune goddesses* who run the team and apparently the school with their wicked charm, of which no one can stand, and yet everybody secretly wants to be a part of. Sounds like your typical power bitches.

"Michelle Miller, Emily Morgan, Lexy Bakova," Brielle spits their names out like curses. They have that ripped from the pages of an expensive magazine look written all over them. And I'm guessing the set of matching scowls is their signature smirk.

"Nice to meet you." I manufacture a smile.

"Natalie Coleman, Kate Winston." Brielle concludes the introductions with a set of homelier girls with bright friendly faces—Natalie with her rust colored ringlets and Kate as pale as paper.

It's uncomfortably quiet, save for a few shy hellos from the last two. The trio of wickedness glares over at me with a special brand of callousness I've yet to encounter. A sense of vulnerability washes over me, and suddenly I'm self-conscious of everything right down to my breathing.

"Hey," a booming voice calls from the side.

With lightning quick strides Logan appears next to me, swooping his arm across my shoulder like it belonged there—not that I'm protesting.

"Trying out for the team?" He's sporting a half-shirt, worn out grey sweats and has a football helmet tucked under his arm.

"Yeah, I think so." I don't tell him that I'm in. That they'll give me Chloe's spot if I want it. I don't want to see his amber eyes smolder with anger at the mention of her name.

He's far more attractive than he was yesterday, and I'm not entirely sure how that's even possible.

"Morning," I say as though magically we were the only two people on the field.

"Morning," he counters, soft as a whisper. He smiles into me with his eyes lighting up like beautiful flames.

I keep staring at her and I'm gonna have a really big problem right here, right now. I hear him say.

I bite down a smile, fighting back the laugh trying to rumble out of my chest. I can feel the heat stinging my cheeks an embarrassing shade of scarlet.

God—I think I'm in love.

His eyes widen with pleasure.

Love? He looks right at me as he says it in his mind.

My eyes widen with horror as I jump free from his grasp.

Shit!

He heard me.

I heard him and he heard me.

Judging by the shocked expression on his face. He didn't expect it either.

4

Listen

Later that night, I watch mesmerized as the trees appear and disappear in and out of the fog as Brielle races us down the narrow streets of Paragon.

Mom was so tired, there was hardly any fight left in her when I asked if I could go to a party tonight. Mom's only concession was that I let Drake tag along. She wants him to get acclimated before school starts. She and Tad are afraid he'll have a hard time fitting in. I wanted to tell her that most likely he won't fit in anyway—primates usually don't fare so well at public school. But I paid the piper and issued Drake a get-out-of-the-house-free-card instead.

"Ellis Harrison is sort of a dick," Brielle says, turning down the music in her bright red Jeep.

Earlier she informed both my mother and me that he came from old money, that he lived in one of the biggest homes in Paragon Estates, a gated community not too far away.

She recites his name to the security guard at the tower who lazily punches in a code and the wooden arm in front of the car rises to let us through.

The Paragon Estates feels far more open, more spacious than the quasi track housing the rest of the island is subject to. We glide down a mysterious winding path flanked with tall blue ponderosa pines lining the periphery. You can feel the affluence just driving past the sprawling homes, each one more extravagant than the last, hiding behind neatly trimmed bushes that nestle their borders. A white bridal fence stretches out alongside the road for what feels like miles as giant eucalyptus shag their leaves into the wind.

The dark velvet night glows an eerie shade of purple, the color of a storybook world, a fairytale. Even through the thick rolling fog you can make out the crystal expanse of stars glinting above. They sparkle down their glory like shards of broken glass.

Brielle pulls into a long stone-paved driveway that widens until it reaches a monolithic estate lit up like a jewel. A giant chandelier glitters out from the second story window just above a set of glass doors adorned with wrought iron. The whole place has a Spanish villa feel, equipped with an enormous three-tiered fountain in the middle of the circular driveway. The base of the manmade spring is surrounded by an entire pride of stone lions. The water illuminates an unearthly glow, and it occurs to me while taking in all of the majesty that I could never get used to living in a place as fantastic as this. I'd have to wear ball gowns to bed and pearls to breakfast. Hell, I'd probably have to *eat* pearls for breakfast.

"Holy shit," Drake hisses as we get out of the Jeep.

The entire upper portion of the driveway is bombarded with cars. I look around suspiciously, trying to decode which one Logan might drive, or Gage for that matter. Speaking of which, I'm not particularly looking forward to seeing the mind reader in question tonight. I still haven't had the chance to properly

27

process what happened this afternoon. He didn't say a word after the strange incident, just took off for practice like a bat out of hell.

Maybe it was my imagination? Maybe I only *thought* he could hear me? Honest to God I'd die if he could. Proclaiming my love for someone, on this, the second day of our acquaintance, is enough to spook anybody. And the last thing I want to do is spook Logan Oliver.

Brielle leads us in through the front door without knocking.

It's noisy inside. My chest picks up the bass from some rap song I don't recognize as an army of shadows laugh and sway to the beat. I don't say anything about the music blowing out my eardrums. I just follow the scarf of Bree's perfume into the next room, which is scarcely illuminated by the residual light from the entry.

It's not wall to wall bodies like the parties I've been to back home, but then those houses were the size of a shoebox, and come to think of it, if we shrunk this place down to size, it would probably be wall to wall bodies, too.

"Ellis!" She flings her arms around a tall, good-looking guy with sandy hair and a deep dimple in his right cheek. My stomach gives a hot pinch at the sight of him. "This is Skyla," Brielle shouts over the music, "and her brother!" She pulls Drake over and laps her arm around his waist.

Ellis doesn't hesitate to offer me a full-blown hug. His hands ride up and down my back like a pair of rabid snakes, nearly unhooking my bra in the process and something tells me that might have been the point. "Nice to meet you." He slithers to my hand and shakes it.

Damn, she's hot. I want to...

I snatch my hand back before the visual has a chance to take over. Some thoughts just aren't worth hearing.

"Look who decided to join the party?" A voice emanates from behind.

Gage appears next to Brielle. His eyes shine bright as beacons as if he's got a blue flashlight in the back of each one. He introduces himself to Drake by way of a high-five.

Gage looks sharp in a stark white polo. It gives off an eerie glow in this low light and matches the white of his teeth.

I press out a quiet smile. Innately I can tell he's sweet. He has a warmth about him, something that every part of me wants to gravitate toward, but it's the prospect of seeing Logan that has my heart racing.

They're a package deal, right? Living together, the bowling alley, football team...

I turn and startle to find him behind me.

"Hey," he says it low, seductive. He folds his arms across his chest and shifts into a defiant stance. The shadows in the room play with his features, sharpening his already cutting good looks, and I can't tell whether or not he's happy to see me.

Brielle pulls Logan over with robust enthusiasm and introduces Drake as my brother. So much for pretending I don't recognize him as a species. At least he's not picking his nose. For that I can be thankful.

Drake reaches up and scratches at the side of his nostril, giving me a mild heart attack in the process.

"You shoot pool?" Logan directs the question at me as though we were the only people in the room.

"I'll break some balls with you guys." Ellis nods into the offer.

"No thanks." Logan doesn't waver from our stare. A tiny smile plays on his lips but he won't give it. Logan and his splendor manage to deafen all of the noise from the room. His eyes seem to have garnered the ability to steal the light from the chandelier, cast it out at the world as though it were their own.

Without a word, I follow Logan through a pair of French doors that lead out to the side yard.

The air outside is perfumed with night blooming jasmine, a scent that reminds me of my backyard in L.A. It coats me with a heavy feeling of nostalgia and I want to escape it, leave the bookmark from the past in another state entirely. Instead, I try to focus on the fog as it deposits its damp residue over my face with its cold ragged breath.

Logan walks us down a dirt trail leading to a barn-like structure in the rear of the property.

"It's warm inside. I promise." He presses his fingers against the small of my back, holding open the door to the miniature house.

It is warm inside, cozy, unlike the mausoleum we left.

He turns on a light in a kitchen the size of the one I had in L.A. In fact it looks surprisingly like a normal sized home with the exception its just one large room with a pool table smack in the middle.

I run my fingers over the smooth red velvet lining the table while Logan fishes the balls out of the pockets and rolls them on top. I watch as he gathers them, places them into the wooden triangle with great patience. He doesn't say a word, just goes about his business like he was at work.

A weirdness has cropped up between us, and I'm staring to think sequestering myself with him so soon wasn't the best idea.

"So," he begins, "how long have you known?" He pushes a stick in my direction as if it were an olive branch.

"Known what?"

He's not talking about love, right? We literally just met and he can't read minds so the whole idea is absurd.

His head ticks to the side, examining me openly under the soft glow of light.

"That I like to play pool?" I tease. I don't tell him I'm a novice at the sport, that I can count on one hand the number of times I've played and still have fingers left over. Instead, I lean in and shoot the white ball across the table and say, "Stripes."

Logan steps in, pinning me against the table with his body over mine. He leans in and shoots from behind my back. Heat emanates off his skin, hot as a summer sidewalk. His knee presses into my thigh like an invitation, and I break out in an unexpected sweat.

"Solids," his warm breath hums across my cheek.

I twist around, landing us nose to nose.

Logan gives a sorrowful smile as his eyes glaze over with lust. He brushes his fingers across the back of my neck and holds me there softly.

Kiss me, he instructs. His eyes widen at the prospect.

A dull moan gets trapped in my throat as I lean in and press my lips against his, soft as a summer breeze.

A small part of me tries to scramble my thoughts, erase the overzealous elation from my being, but I can't. I grab the back of his neck and push him in deeper, indulging in a kiss that goes on for miles. His tongue darts around my mouth, glides across my teeth, happy to be there.

Logan pushes me back onto the pool table and the balls shoot out from underneath me. He runs his lips over my face, my neck, igniting me with a wave of quick kisses. He pulses up to my ear before crashing over my lips, perfect and hungry.

Right here. Right now, he purrs.

"What?" I slap my hands against his chest, pushing him off with a violent force.

"Sorry." His hands fly through the air quick as a stickup.

"I better go." I bolt from the pool house and into the night.

If I stayed another minute I might have said yes.

5

Questions

Ellis' party is still going strong.

Brielle is nowhere to be seen and suspiciously neither is Drake. The disgusting possibilities float through my mind—welcome as a school of dead fish.

"Skyla," Logan's deep voice emanates from behind as I peer into the kitchen.

I ignore him briefly as I spy on Brielle and Drake pushed up against the sink. He's busy raking his hands up and down her back octopus-style, and I find the entire display of mollusk-like affection difficult to watch.

I lean back into the hall filled with disbelief.

"I think we need to talk," Logan shakes his head when he says it. He looks serious as though a major infraction just occurred.

"Look," the strange urge to cry infiltrates me, "I just really want to go home." My knees tremble as I try to steady myself against the wall. The idea of someone else having the same ability more than freaks me out. Especially when it's a boy I happen to like.

"Let me take you," he says it soft and gentle as if trying to convince me there's nothing to fear, as if reading peoples minds, Drake getting it on with the super model next door, were as normal as breathing.

I follow Logan outside, afraid to hold his hand or touch him in general. If he can hear my thoughts that means the deformity that lives in me also lives in him. That it wasn't some random gift bestowed upon me and my father—that others have this, too.

Maybe I gave it to Logan like a cold or mono? Maybe I have the ability to pass it to the ones I love, or at least those I believe I do.

We make our way down the winding driveway, past the rows of expensive cars and into the great expanse of a deep velvet night.

"So, where we going?" My fingers brush up against him and this time I don't fight it. I form my hand around his because it feels natural, because I want to.

He stops short and turns to face me. *I live across the street.* His eyes press into mine.

Can you hear me? I offer it as a test run.

"Yes," he pushes the word out with great intensity.

"Oh God."

He hears me. He knows my thoughts. I wiggle out of his grasp.

Can you hear me now? I offer it with all the sarcastic inflection I can muster.

He pulls his cheek up on one side.

"I need to touch you," he says.

"You're just like me," I marvel. All the anger and confusion vanishes like smoke and suddenly I'm thrilled to have Logan

Oliver standing before me. Somehow, someway, we found our way to each other.

"And you're just like me, but prettier." He leans in slow and sears me with a kiss.

The world shifts, the lavender sky spreads its wings over the two of us like a blessing.

We continue the meandering walk over to his house. It mirrors Ellis' home in width, but the styling is different, more rambling ranch than Spanish Villa. The lights are all off, and I wait on the porch as he literally pops in and out to grab his keys and wallet. He leads me over to an oversized white truck and helps me climb inside. I text Drake and let him know where I'm headed.

"You really want to go home?" He asks, settling himself in his seat. He sticks the keys in the ignition, and the truck roars to life beneath us.

"Not really," the thought of hanging out with Mom and Tad is enough to make me fashion a noose out of my hair. "You wanna just drive?"

"Sure, I know just the place to take you."

Take me? God—it's probably some dense forest where the locals go to mate.

"I know I'm from L.A. and stuff," I start, "so you probably think I've been everywhere—done everything," I haven't dropped in a hole, and that's something I'd like to do right about now, "but I haven't, and I don't plan on it. I'm a... " I stop shy of formulating the word 'virgin' on my lips. We've already determined I'm a freak, well, I guess we both are, but still, no point in dissecting the issue.

"I'm glad you haven't been everywhere," he says it with a disarming charm that makes me writhe on the inside, "or done everything." He glances over with a peaceable smile.

We drive for long stretches in silence. A thicket of boiling clouds canopy across the sky like an oversized umbrella. They press into the island, hiding the moon and the stars like a cloak.

"Do you know what it is?" He asks, taking the turnoff marked Devil's Peak. He pulls into a graveled lot and parks in close to a wooden fence that sits at the edge of the cliff. The moon breaks through and shines its beams down over the water.

"It's so beautiful," I breathe. I'm mesmerized by the glistening river of light as it dances in an erratic line over the waves.

"So are you, but you're evading the question." He picks up my hand and nestles it in his.

Do you know why you're like this?

A breath gets caught in my throat.

A picture of my father—his perfect smile blinks through my mind. Lately each time I think of him it feels as though I've fallen through a trapdoor.

Another image vies for my attention—a young couple, both filled with elation as they hold up an infant between them.

That's me in the middle. Logan looks at me intently.

I'm sorry. My heart breaks for him. *What happened?*

Car accident—so I was told.

"I could do this with my dad." It frightens me to do this with Logan. "My mom, my sister, they can't."

"Gage can't. Look—I just want you to know I don't make a habit of touching people and reading their thoughts."

"I'm impressed." But not sure I'm buying it.

"Are you?" He pulls my fingers to his lips and kisses them individually. "But you don't really know why you can do this, do you." It comes out more a fact than a question.

"No. Will you tell me?"

Logan wraps his arms around me and pulls me close.

I don't fight him because there's nowhere else I'd rather be.

"Yes, I'll tell you," he leans in and brushes his lips against mine, "but not tonight." He crashes his lips over mine with a hot flurry of kisses.

And I don't object.

6

Inquisition

In the late afternoon, when I finally manage to roll out of bed, I head downstairs and find my mother in the kitchen.

"You look like death warmed over." She plucks at my hair as I walk past her on the way to the fridge.

"Gee thanks." I pull out the O.J. and lean against the island.

"You ever miss Daddy?" It comes out childlike, simple.

Her eyes widen then retract as she glances back down at her game of Sudoku. I recognize the small book she purchased at the gas station before leaving L.A.

"Only like crazy," her voice dips to a guilty whisper. It's usually an indication that Tad is somewhere in the vicinity. I hate the way my father has become some dirty little secret ever since Tad crashed into our lives. It's like a sin to acknowledge my father even existed.

I don't know if it's the fact I could have easily slept another six hours, or the fact I can't stand Tad in general but my blood begins to percolate, brewing itself into a perfect hormonal rage.

"It's OK to talk about him, you know," I say a little louder than necessary. "I wasn't exactly hatched from an egg. He put me here." The idea of my parents copulating sprints through my mind, takes my appetite out along with it.

"Nobody said you were hatched from an egg." She gives the slight hint of annoyance. "Spare us the attitude. Looks like someone got up on the wrong side of the bed."

I slam down the carafe in my hand, hard on the counter.

"Do I have to get up on the wrong side of the bed to think about Dad?"

"Skyla." Mom's eyes close heavy with regret.

Already we've started this day—this crazy train, down the wrong track.

"Excuse me but I still remember him," my voice shakes as I deliver the words a little louder than anticipated. Without thinking I walk over and clutch my hands over her bare shoulders. "I miss him." Tears stream down my cheeks as I dig my nails into her. *Can you hear me? Tell me if you can hear me. Explain to me what the hell this is, because he's dead, and he can't tell me anything anymore!*

"Skyla," she shrieks, trying to break free from my hold. "Tad...*Tad?*" She bucks against me in an effort to wrangle away. *Tad's right, she's going off the deep end because I never took her to therapy. God—what if she's on drugs?*

I let go as if her skin were on fire. She nurses her arms, holds herself tenderly as Tad the step monkey fast approaches.

"That's it," he barks. "You've gone too far, Skyla," he reprimands while inspecting my mother's injuries.

My mother breaks down into heaving sobs. He encapsulates her in his arms as she murmurs something, and he rocks her like soothing a baby.

I don't hang out to watch the rest of the show. Instead, I speed out the front door and slam it with a bionic force. It goes off like a shotgun blast, ricocheting through the virginal morning air. Birds jet out of the pine branches and fly away from the house. I watch as they trek across the sky, quick as a dart.

I wish I could be that free.

Barefoot, with messy hair and no make-up is hardly the first impression you want to make on the parents of your new best friend.

Brielle lets me in, still wiping the sleep from her eyes. She takes in all my I-just-rolled-out-of-bed glory and blinks back surprise.

"Casual," she nods, "I like that."

The house is heavy with the sweet woodsy scent of bacon. I haven't had real bacon since Tad came into our lives and declared pig-fried flesh something akin to an abomination.

A tall blonde with short-cropped hair and a friendly face peers over Brielle's shoulder.

"You must be Skyla." She puts out a slender hand, and I shake it.

"Nice to meet you," I say.

"Darla," she says giving my hand a firm squeeze. "Have you eaten yet?"

"Oh, that's OK." I shake my head. Like it's not bad enough I've come to their door disheveled, I need to eat their food, too.

"I insist." Brielle threads her arm through mine. "Our friendship isn't official until you break bread with me—or pancakes." She winks over at her mom like maybe they're poison.

Brielle's house is decorator perfect, all done up in shabby chic. It's covered with a dozen different toile fabrics, from curtains, to throw pillows. Every square inch has been gift wrapped in repeating patterns. And knick-knacks abound in every nook and cranny, yet it doesn't feel cluttered. Personally, I'd love it if Mom saw fit to unleash a pastel fabric bomb in the Landon household. I'd be in heaven if my bedroom looked exactly like this right down to the blue chandelier hanging over the center of the dining room table. Tad and Drake however would definitely feel their manhood disintegrating at the speed of light in an atmosphere like this.

"Your dad at work?" I ask Bree while her mother dishes up breakfast.

"Probably. They're divorced," she pauses, "I have a sister at Washington State. It's just me and my mom right now."

"That's right. Just us girls," she sings back with a slight country accent.

I wish my mother were secure enough to live on her own. I tried to talk her out of marrying Tad—being *near* Tad. Something about him sends a chill up my spine, sharp as razors. But I could never put my finger on why, and thus have never built an adequate case against him. Who am I kidding? She would have married him anyway. I'm the last person on the planet my mother would consult for the color of her pedicure, let alone marriage.

ADDISON MOORE

"You have fun at the party last night?" Brielle knocks her knee into mine beneath the table like she's speaking in code.

"Logan drove me home. Showed me the overlook." I shrug trying to ignore the fact I'm blushing ten shades of red.

"Overlook?" Darla lays our plates down and takes a seat. "Pretty girl like you? I bet he showed more than the overlook," she draws the words out suggestively.

My mouth falls open at the sexual implications of it all. God, I hope she means landscape or the shiny blue Pacific. But I bet not. Brielle obviously has one of those 'special' moms that thinks sex at sixteen is natural as breathing. I'm pretty sure I'd never in a million years want my mom to convert to Darla's special brand of parenting philosophy. The thought of my mother talking to me about sex makes me want to stab my eyes out with a fork, gouge even deeper and scramble my brains to prevent the conversation from ever happening.

"He showed me Ellis Harrison's pool house. It looks like a barn." It comes out unnatural as though I were lying.

Darla explodes into a fit of laughter. She picks up her plate and heads out of the room like I had chased her out with my sheer stupidity.

"A *barn*? Is that what they're calling it these days?" She cries from the other room.

"She's gone." Brielle shakes her head in disgust. Maybe she doesn't appreciate a 'cool' mom either.

"So, anyway," I pat my bacon with a napkin, "that's what happened. How was your night?"

"Awesome with a capital everything." She takes a sip of her milk while batting her clumped lashes.

"I hope it was awesome because you had a good time for reasons other than Count Drakeula." It's not my fault he comes equipped with sharp pointy teeth—that and the fact I'm not above name-calling.

"Count Drakeula can suck my blood anytime he wishes."

"You know I'm more than grossed out by this. You should go for Gage. He's like a Greek god or something." My stomach pinches with jealousy as if to protest the idea.

"Been there, tried to do that. Besides, he was talking about *you* last night. It doesn't faze him at all that Logan practically staked his claim."

"Me?" Something deep inside me purrs at the thought of Gage the claim jumper interested in me. I've never been the center of attention before, and for sure not from boys of this caliber. "It's hard to believe they don't already have girlfriends."

"They really haven't gone out with anyone since Chloe. They took her death pretty hard. We all did." The smile bleeds off her face. She traces the rim of her glass with her fingertip as a spontaneous show of tears wobble inside her lids.

There's so much mystery surrounding Chloe.

"Tell me all about her. I really want to know."

7

Eulogy

Brielle bleeds words as fast as she can speak them. We head up to her bedroom, which is done up in yet another fit of pink toile. It becomes embarrassingly apparent they've safely exceeded their legal limit of both pink and toile in this household. They're taking this whole, *we are women, see our décor* thing a bit too far. I'll have to bring Mia and Melissa up here sometime and watch them swoon. I'm sure as soon as Taddy dearest hears of their newfound lust for a replica bedroom he'll be on it in one pinky twisted minute. Not only is Melissa a daddy's girl, but he's taken Mia under his wing by proxy. I won't deny the fact I'm insanely jealous. I used to be a daddy's girl myself, but now there's no more daddy.

A stream of tears rolls down my cheek as I listen to Brielle ramble on about how great Chloe was. Only my tears aren't for Chloe and her albeit brief life, in fact, sadly, I sort of feel like I'm actually detesting her by the minute even though it's totally not cool to detest a dead person. My tears are solely for my father—my father who's been allocated to a mere whisper in Tad Landon's glass castle. My father who used to take me to the pier to gaze out at the open night sky and point to the stars saying that's where we came from, where we really belong.

Brielle chats incessantly about her dead BFF as we get ready for cheer, and as we face my parents and I spill an apology about my behavior earlier—lying like spilling oil. She talks as I shower, while I change for practice, and on the way over in the car.

"Anyway, one day I'll have to show you all the scrapbooks. We used to sit around and piece them together at night. Pretty lame, right?"

"No, I think that's great you have all those memories laid out to look at. I wish I had something like that of my dad. All our pictures are still floating around on my hard drive." For so long I could barely think of him. Seeing his pictures in the hall of our old house killed me on an intimate level. I used to wish my mother would cover them up—burn them. And now there aren't any around. Tad came in and hijacked our lives. We moved, and those are the only things my mother has yet to unpack.

For a moment I consider turning my room into a shrine for my father. That alone might ensure the fact Mom and Tad would never set foot in it. Then again, neither would I.

We pull into the school parking lot covered with the pall of another grey day.

"I like the weather here," I say, letting the moist film adhere to my face, my open palms, as I drink it in.

"No one likes the weather here, except maybe the vampires." She knocks into me with her shoulder and gives a wild cackle.

Natalie and Kate catch up with us before we hit the field. Natalie's stiff curls are pulled back into a bumpy ponytail. Kate looks fresh out of the shower with dripping wet hair, long blonde strands as thick as spaghetti.

Brielle laments the fact practice is so early even though it's nearly three in the afternoon. "One thing's for sure," she brushes up against my shoulder when she says it, "Ellis Harrison knows how to throw a party."

I avert my gaze in the event she wants to drag this conversation back to the gutter like her mother did and spot Logan from across the field with his hands on his hips. He stands perfectly still as the rest of the football teams runs wild in some well-orchestrated play.

I wave over to him with a spastic enthusiasm and catch his attention. He lifts his hand just as a wall of a bodies lunge at him. Logan lands flat on his back, three bodies deep, and I let out a groan at the sight.

"Looks like your hands are lethal weapons." Kate mimics my wave.

"Very funny," I say as we make our way over the expanse of emerald lawn.

It feels good to have friends, or the prospective friends at least. It feels more than good to have the prospect of a boyfriend even though he's not officially my anything. And it's especially good that he shares my secret, that we can do it together. It brings a whole new meaning to a meeting of the minds.

"Alright bitches!" Michelle barks out at us. Her face is a thing of beauty but her personality clouds any physical perfection she might have. "Ready begin!" She blares music from a boom box without waiting for us to get into position. I try to copy the steps and keep up, but it's pointless. I'm more than ten steps behind everyone else at any given time.

I bump into Lexy Bakova as I foolishly attempt a running kick and end up knocking her to the ground by way of my foot.

"Shit!" I cover my mouth.

The music stops abruptly as the triune goddesses quickly descend upon her.

"I'm so sorry." I crouch down, trying to catch a glimpse of the unintended victim of my clumsiness. "It was an accident, I swear."

A powerful blow explodes over my mouth, sends me flying backward onto the lawn. It takes a second for me to realize it was Emily's elbow that so violently decided to connect with my dental work.

"Oh, I'm *so* sorry," she exaggerates the words.

"It was an accident, I swear," Michelle bleats it out with sarcasm. They break out in a fit of cackles while helping Lexy to her feet.

"What the fuck!" Kate shouts as she helps me up. Natalie and Brielle look equally pissed for me and I'd appreciate this a whole lot more if I wasn't dying in pain.

"You're bleeding." Brielle wipes my mouth with the back of her hand, and a smear of red liquid streaks across her finger.

I inventory my teeth by way of my tongue to see if I've lost any in the process. I can taste the salt in my blood—tastes like rust, like I've been sucking on old pennies and I spit before the urge to vomit takes over.

"You're so sick," Lexy reprimands with her hand still flat over her stomach.

"Excuse me," Brielle charges at her, "she almost had her teeth rearranged, you stupid bitch!"

"Who asked you to join the squad anyway?" Lexy doesn't hesitate baring her fangs in my direction.

"I did." Brielle takes an aggressive step forward. A small gust of wind pumps up her hair like a lions mane, and for a second I'm afraid a catfight is about to break out. "You gotta problem with that?"

"Actually," Michelle steps between the two of them, "we all have a problem with that." She fixes those expressionless black eyes on me with venom. "You think you can move into Chloe's house, take her spot on the team, steal her boyfriend, and call it a day?"

"If you really want to be like her," Emily bites down a wicked grin, "why don't you swan dive off Devil's Peak?" Flames shoot out of Emily's eyes as if she has the power to will it to happen. But the details are worn. You don't swan dive then bury yourself in a shallow grave. If she were really Chloe's friend, she would never have gone there in the first place.

Brielle pushes into Emily's chest, hard with both hands.

"Shit!" Emily screams at top volume before doubling over. "I think you popped an implant."

"That's it," Michelle snaps, "practice is canceled."

Lexy crashes into my shoulder as she strides on by. "You better watch your back, bitch."

8

Lust and Things

Brielle takes me to the nearest ER, and I blatantly refuse to get out of the car. Instead, we end up someplace where the attendants have bodies strong enough to protect you from a nuclear missile and can heal you with their good looks alone— the bowling alley.

I'm beginning to appreciate the aggressive flicker of light as we make our way inside. I love how spacious the bowling alley is, how the heavenly scent of buttered popcorn might actually be breeding air born calories.

In less than a minute, Logan gently pats my cheek with a bag of crushed ice. Every now and again he pulls it back to inspect the damage.

I place my hand over his arm—caress it back and forth until I can hear him clearly.

You'll live. He gives a bleak smile. *Stay away from those girls. They're mostly trouble.*

They said I stole Chloe's boyfriend. Did I? My cheeks explode with color.

I'm shocked by my own audacity.

He gives a gentle laugh.

"What's up with all the star gazing and silence?" Brielle looks genuinely perturbed. "If you die in your sleep because you have a concussion, it's literally on your head, missy."

"Points to you for sounding like my mother." I trail down Logan's arm and clasp onto his fingers.

Brielle glares at me a moment before excusing herself to the bathroom.

Was it something I said? I give a sarcastic smile.

"Look," Gage blows it out in disgust, "if you guys are going to do this, find a booth in the back where people can't see you," The slight hint of jealousy lingers long after leaves.

Are you sure Gage can't do this? I mean, you are related, I ask.

No. He knows all about it. Wouldn't take my hand if it meant getting out of a fire. He's mastered other tricks though, far more useless, I assure you.

What do you mean, other tricks? Logan, tell me what this is. Is it some sort of genetic defect? Why can I do this? Why do we have this ability?

His face sours. He pulls his hand away and drops it under the table.

"I want to. Not here though."

"Why not? Nobody will know. We can do it in secret."

"Really?" Brielle laughs as she takes a seat, her hand stuffed with a giant wad of tissue. "Why not right here on the table? I don't think anyone will notice at all."

"Not that," I balk. "Are you OK?" Her eyes are puffy and swollen like she's just had a good cry. All this talk about Chloe must have really upset her. I hate the thought I was somehow responsible. It was me who brought her up.

"It's just hard sometimes." She looks up at Logan. "Chloe's been on my mind, and it's gone from bad to worse."

"Chloe was your friend." He squints like he doesn't really mean it. "It's OK to miss her."

My chest sinks like a stone when he says her name.

"I know." Brielle wipes the tears and looks over at me. "She did have the bad habit of hanging out with Em, Michelle, and Lexy. They weren't always the triune anything. She was the one who tempered them, and now without her they've gone feral. It's like their wickedness unleashed the second Chloe disappeared."

"Disappeared?" Of course she disappeared. I just never thought of it that way. In my mind it had all happened backward with her already lying in state in her casket.

"She went missing for two weeks," Brielle whispers it like a secret. "Nobody knows what happened. Coroner says her body was thrashed when they found her," she lowers her lashes, "she had these strange cuts all over." Brielle gazes out past the lanes, through the walls, and straight into Chloe's grave.

"Cuts? Maybe they were scrapes from branches? Like she was trying to escape," I offer.

Logan shakes his head as though trying to evict the visual from his mind.

"Deep incisions," Brielle's voice breaks when she says it. "Her mom said it looked barbaric like she was used as some kind of science experiment. They think maybe somebody tortured her," her voice rasps to nothing.

"Dear God." I mouth the words.

Logan pulls the bag of ice away and shifts its contents before gently replacing it to my lip.

I had no idea about Chloe. I'm starting to regret ever asking about her. For all I know the killer could have extricated her from our shared bedroom in the middle of the night. They could have a perverse desire to snatch girls from that exact location again and again. I don't really know anyone here on Paragon that well. For all I know he could be lurking somewhere right here in the bowling alley—watching me, waiting.

For sure I need to give my brain something fresh to gnaw on so I change the subject.

"Listen, if I can convince my parents to have a party will you come?" It may not be the perfect segue, but it beats ruminating on a killer.

"Of course." A devilish smile play on Logan's lips. Although I doubt a party was the venue he had in mind to let me in on his big secret—our secret.

"I mean just you guys and," I look over at Brielle, "Drake will be there. Kate and Nat can come. My mom has this thing about my stepbrother meeting people. I know she'll be OK with it." Never mind the fact I almost clawed her flesh off this morning. I'm sort of hoping she's already long forgotten about that.

"Sounds good." Logan picks up my hand. *But I can't tell you in a room full of people. We need to be alone—just you and me.*

Tell me now. No one will know.

Alone.

Am I going to freak out when I hear it?

He doesn't say anything. Not a single thought sails through his mind.

You don't think I can handle it, do you? I ask.

It's not that I don't think you can't handle it. Once you realize who you are, you won't ever get a chance to go back.

Who am I?

Skyla.

Not funny. I don't scare easy.

You're lying. He gives a bleak smile.

You're saying it'll frighten me?

It will and it should.

9

Speechless

"And think about Drake," I motion over to him sprawled across the sectional, "he could meet all kinds of people who go to West Paragon." I nod convincingly into my mother.

Brielle and I have spent the last several minutes building our case for a simple movie night with friends tomorrow night. Just the sheer heft of how hard it is convincing her to have a few people over, you would think we were asking to sacrifice kittens at midnight.

"I'm all for it," she gives a dismissive wave, "I'll take Tad out for a surprise date and catch the ten o'clock show. Fair enough?"

"What about the girls?" I hadn't even thought of Mia and Melissa until they walked past us five seconds ago.

"They'll come with." She relaxes into the idea.

"Really?" A small squeal of delight escapes, and I'm careful to check it. No need to let her in on the fact I'm beyond excited. Just the thought of having Logan over makes me want to bounce like a three-year old.

"We've still got boxes everywhere and don't think it hasn't gone unnoticed that you haven't exactly been digging into them."

"I swear," I hold my hand in the air like a girl scout, "I will tackle those boxes come Sunday morning."

"Nice try, but I'm dragging the whole lot of you to church."

Brielle gives an audible laugh.

"It wouldn't hurt if you joined us," Mom offers.

"Thanks, but no thanks." Brielle averts her eyes when my mother's not looking. Once my mom has a chance to get to know Darla, I think she'll realize they have polarizing parental opinions and I'm betting marital ones, too.

When my dad was alive, church was a part of the family. It was mostly something my dad encouraged and none of us protested too severely. But since my mother married the antichrist, none of us have even stepped near hallowed ground.

"OK, Sunday afternoon," I submerge my glee like trying to hold an air bubble underwater, "and we won't make a mess. You'll see."

"Bitch squad, three o' clock." Brielle pushes me into the clearance rack at the mall.

I hadn't really thought about clothes before, but after ransacking my closet it was clear there was nothing Logan worthy to wear tomorrow night.

"Would you stop?" I say, trying to right myself. "I'm not afraid of them." I watch as Michelle, Lexy and Emily turn their noses up at the meager offerings. "If they hate everything so damn much maybe *they* should jump off Devil's Peak." A part of me can't believe I just said that out loud. I keep forgetting that comments like that bring up the pain of Chloe's death. It's embarrassing how many times I've emotionally slit Brielle's wrist with my tongue and let her bleed with grief. "Sorry," I whisper as the three of them head in our direction.

"No offense taken." Brielle pretends to interest herself in an ugly striped sweater.

"So, Michelle," Emily ups the volume of her ultra annoying voice, "you give Logan back his sweater yet?"

I look up. It's like hearing his name inspires some kind of kneejerk reaction in me. And why would she have his sweater? Probably just bullshit.

"I haven't seen him yet." Michelle glowers briefly in my direction. "It was just last night he left it in my room." They break out in a fit of laughter. The sound of their voices erodes the peace and quiet of the store, fills my ears with its chaffing rhythm. I can tell by their expressions, making me miserable offers them a unique brand of nirvana.

Emily makes her way over in a series of heavy plods. Her dark curls frame her face, harsh and unattractive. It reminds me of a picture I once saw of a mermaid who had her locks shorn by the sea witch. When I was little, my father would read me fairytales at bedtime and I would study the pictures, dream about them. I used to wish I could be like that girl, jump into the sea and swim with the fishes, live in that magical underwater world.

"I guess I owe you an apology." Her watery blue eyes drill into mine.

I'm stupefied by the notion of an apology—struck without words. Emily Morgan, the evil mermaid, eating crow? Doubtful.

"I guess you didn't steal everything from Chloe." Emily steps away as Lexy replaces her in the line up.

"How does it feel to be sleeping in the same room that Logan did Chloe in? Has he done you there too? You know, it being familiar stomping grounds and all. He is known for being insatiable in that department, isn't that right Michelle?"

"I don't kiss and tell, Lex." A slow spreading smile widens across Michelle's face.

It's like I see her for the first time, her dark honeyed skin, eyes black as midnight, her lips naturally pulled in a snarl whether the occasion warrants it or not. Her hair falls down in burnt amber waves well past her shoulders. She holds a wicked beauty. I could see guys lining up around the block to take a ride if she threw out the offer. But I'm not buying that Logan is one of them.

"Let's go," I whisper to Bree.

"Not so fast." Michelle steps out in front of me. "Logan says you're having a party tomorrow night. So I guess that means we're invited, right?" She clogs up the air with her sarcastic drivel.

"Really? Logan told you that?" I bet she vomits lies in her sleep.

"Yup. He says it's going to be really exciting, what with all the movies and popcorn." Michelle digs into me with a look of satisfaction. "Oh wait, he didn't mention popcorn—guess it won't be exciting after all."

"Oh, I know," Emily interjects. "We can all go to the library first and check out books. Then we can snuggle up on the couch together and read them round robin style."

They explode with laughter.

"Better yet," Emily continues, "we can do personality makeovers!" She's laughing so hard, tears streak down the side of her face, bleaching out her foundation in jagged white tracks.

Brielle grabs me by the elbow and rushes us out the door, setting the security alarm off in the process. She looks down at the ugly striped sweater in her hand before tossing it back into the store, nailing Michelle in the face with it.

"If any of that crap about Logan is true, his ass is toast," Brielle hisses.

If any of that stuff about Logan is true I want off Paragon.

I'll swim all the way back to L.A. if I have to.

10

Gathering

"So it's prolly the wrong time to ask, but how exactly does one garner a handful of enemies in the short time we've been here?" Drake asks with a mouthful of food.

I slap the next chip out of his hand.

"Stay away from the rations," I snip. "It's not for you."

To say I've been a little pissy since my confrontation yesterday with the bitch squad is a gross miscarriage of the truth. I've been a *lot* pissy, and stabby and all around miserable.

I made Brielle promise she wouldn't tell me whatever info she may have gleaned from her shift at the bowling alley. I want to hear it right out of Logan's mouth—see his face when he tells me what exactly went on with Michelle. Hopefully nothing.

A thousand different scenarios have played out in my mind and the truth is not one of them made me feel better. And the thought of Logan having sex with some dead girl in my bedroom sent me packing for the downstairs couch last night. I know she wasn't dead at the time, but dead or alive, it hurt like hell to hear it.

"Please," Brielle snorts into Drake. She sounds just as annoyed with him as I do. Maybe the delusion has been shattered, and she sees him for the monkey boy he really is. "They're everybody's enemies."

"So you're saying I'm in good company." I stir the lemonade in a large glass pitcher my mother uses for parties. Chips and dip? Lemonade? "This is so going to suck."

"No it's not." Brielle pushes me aside and continues to stir for me. "We're watching a movie. The guys are bringing pizza. And by nights end you may not hate Michelle so much."

My eyes dart over to her accusingly. She's implying that what Michelle said yesterday was true, at least in part. I hold up my hand. I don't want to hear another word—for now.

"When they get here, I'll take Logan upstairs and make him tell me everything. Just start the movie—don't bother waiting for us. I've seen it a thousand times already."

"Knew it," Drake balks. "This 'innocent get together' is a rouse for you to get it on with some guy in your bedroom." He looks rather proud of his misinformed epiphany.

At least Mom and Tad have already left with the girls in tow, which leaves me free to beat the shit out of Drake should the need arise and God knows it's arising as we speak.

The doorbell goes off.

"Saved by the bell," I say, speeding past him, "literally."

Brielle whisks by and lets them in. Gage strides in with a giant white pizza box, digging his dimples in my direction as if there were romantic implications behind those deep wells. Natalie and Kate come in all smiles and hellos, each offering a hug.

"I can't believe they did that to you," Kate whispers. Actually, I'm not sure which offense she's referencing. The list seems to grow by the minute.

Logan holds up the rear. He looks luminescent with a crisp white t-shirt, inky dark jeans—the scent of his cologne offering me a warm embrace before he ever reaches me. Track marks linger in his hair, still damp around the edges from the shower.

"Hi." He gives a soft embrace rubbing the skin on the back of my neck with his fingers. *I'm innocent I swear.* He presses out a sweet smile that I could never convict him with.

"I believe you." Something about Logan has the power to render me spellbound in his presence. Even if we didn't share our gift I would be anyway.

We gather in the family room where I toss paper plates like Frisbees. Logan doesn't eat, just stands off to the side with his arms folded across his chest as if he were waiting for his trial.

"So here's the DVD," I say, handing it over to Gage. "If you don't like it blame Drake." It's some cheesy movie from like ten years ago. I point over to the cabinet beneath the TV. "There's lots more crap where that came from." That was Tad's major contribution to the household—a boatload of B movies.

"You get the comedy channel?" Gage takes the remote and channel surfs while everyone finds a spot and gets comfy.

"Hey," I spear a look of feigned surprise over at Logan, "would you like a tour of the house?"

"Why, yes. Yes I would," he matches my playful tone.

"You're going to miss the movie." Kate pinches my shorts as I walk by.

"That's the point." Natalie pulls up a toss pillow and hugs it close to her chest. "They're going to entertain themselves."

Gage looks up. His eyes spear through me like a javelin. There's something searing about that penetrating stare. It makes me want to know all of his secrets and Logan's combined.

"We're just going to talk." I don't know why I felt the need to quantify how I spend my time to Gage of all people, but a small part of me wanted to. It's like he knows me. Like we're connected in some strange way that I don't fully understand. There's so much I don't know. I plan on shaking all of the answers out of Logan in the next few hours. By the time I go to bed tonight, in the same room he supposedly *did* Chloe—I'd better know everything.

"Hey Skyla?" Drake calls out as Logan and I are about to ascend the stairs. "There's a stack of rubbers in my top drawer. Feel free to grab one. I hear it's a safe way to talk to people."

Freaking moron.

11

Truth

I spent all morning cleaning and hiding the things that seem to multiply and run errant in my bedroom when I'm not looking. My bed is perhaps the neatest it's been in its entire wicker-framed history. All of my stuffed animals, as embarrassing as it is to admit, are stowed safely beneath my bed.

I scan the floor for any bras or underwear that may have gone undetected. My clothes are native to the rug in the center of the room, which my mother has lovingly dubbed as the hamper.

The room itself is nothing special, and for sure nothing pretty with stacks of cardboard boxes lining the periphery. The walls are still a dingy white. One day this summer, I for sure want to paint it a really pretty green.

"I'll help."

"Help?" I let go of his hand and bounce over to the mattress, patting the spot right next to me.

"Paint your room."

"Are you kidding?" I bury my head in the pillow.

I was so nervous about having him up here I completely forgot that holding his hand was like inviting him to listen in on my underwear laden monologue.

"And you hid things pretty well." He reaches under the bed and yanks up a prize—the stuffed elephant I won at the county fair when I was eleven.

"Give me that," I laugh, snatching the animal and hugging it hard across my chest. "Don't touch him, he's mine."

"So," he digs his fingers into the hair at the base of my neck, "you want to know why I was at Michelle's." It comes out expressionless.

"It's none of my business where you go." I drift my gaze over to the door—wonder if I locked it.

"I locked it." He smiles.

"No reason to," I say it cold.

"Michelle has something I want."

"I hear most girls do."

"Not that. And no, most girls don't. You do." He cocks his head to the side with a blatant flirtatious smile. "Michelle has something else. Something nobody else could give me."

"What?"

"I can't say."

"Say," I command.

"It's something of Chloe's."

"Who's going to care?"

"You'll care—you may want it." His brows raise a notch. "And I'm pretty sure I'll want to give it to you, at least in part."

"OK," a lungful of air expresses through my lips, "anybody ever tell you, you talk in circles?" I reach over and interlace our fingers. I feel so comfortable sitting on my bed with him. It's strange. "Are you sleeping with Michelle?"

"No."

"Have you slept with Michelle?"

"Almost, but that was months after Chloe died and I was a head case."

"Did you sleep with Chloe in my bedroom?" I shoot the words out with a quick assault.

Our eyes lock, imprisoning one another in a solemn gaze.

"Yes."

I push back a good six inches toward the headboard. Any comfort I may have felt has dissipated quick as a vapor. A million viral things want to stream from my mouth all at once— every single one an excuse to kick him in the face.

He doesn't say anything. Instead he leans back on the bed and covers his eyes with his arm. A soft breath of exasperation blows from his lips.

"It's not like you knew me then." I immediately regret my words. Who am I anyway? I'm just some girl he met. He's probably known Chloe forever. She was probably the love of his life, and if I start a relationship with him now I'll always be competing with a memory. "Just tell me about the touch, how we can hear." All I want from Logan Oliver is for him to spill his deep dark secrets and get the hell out of my bedroom.

He sits up and scoots over, careful not to touch me.

"I think we should do this with words." He touches his lips when he says it.

"Afraid to let me in much?"

He shakes his head.

"More like, afraid to hear you." He sounds out each word with caution, treading lightly so he won't get burned. "It happened twice with Chloe and me. It was stupid. Chloe and

I…" he shakes his head, "she wasn't the right person for me."
He picks up my hand. "By the time she disappeared we had
already broken up, which put me at the top of the suspect list."

Logan is the last person I'd suspect of something like that.

"Tell me what Michelle has," I ask.

"Her diary."

"Oh."

"She left something in it for me." He pulls his lips in a line.
"Anyway, when I get it, you can read it if you like." He takes up
my hand.

I would like that, I say surprising myself with my honesty.
What better way to know the girl who once lived in my room?

He blinks a smile.

"So what about me? This thing?" I don't want to talk about
Chloe anymore, like ever.

He rattles my hand in the air and I take it back.

"This thing. You said your dad did it?"

"Yes. My mom and sister can't."

"Your dad ever talk about his family? Do you know them?"

"Just my grandma. She lives in a nursing home back in L.A.
My mother left her there to rot." Harsh, but true.

"She ever talk about angels?"

"All the time, but she's senile. The doctors said it was one of
her fixations. It was nonstop angels everyday, all the time."

"Well she might not be as senile as everybody thinks. The
only other people that share our gift have Nephilim blood in
them."

"Nephilim?" I pull back to get a better look at him.

"Angels who chose their lust for women over their desire to remain on the frontlines for God. They came down and started families as if they were human."

"Are you saying I'm part Nephilim?"

"I think so, but I'll have to take a small vile of blood to be sure."

"You're kidding, right?" My hearts races at the prospect. "I can't stand the sight of blood."

"Well then, you'd make a lousy vampire." His lips curve just shy of a smile.

"And where do you send this vial? Angels-R-Us?"

"My uncle runs the mortuary. He has access to testing."

"Your uncle runs the mortuary? I thought your family ran the bowling alley." Just the thought of a room full of dead bodies sends a chill up my spine.

"My father owned the bowling alley. My uncle had it under management until he could pass it to me. I've been running it into the ground ever since I was fourteen." He shrugs. "I never claimed to be good at anything."

"Fourteen?"

"I had help. Still do. But back to the topic at hand." He pulls out a lighter, a scalpel, and a small glass vial from out of his pocket. "Are you ready to get the answers you've been looking for?"

12

On Death and Dying

The morgue is quiet and cold. It sits at the northern tip of the island surrounded by churches as though they needed the strength of brick and mortar to shelter the dead. The cemetery lies just behind the mortuary proper with only a few sparse headstones followed by rows of glittering plaques.

I talked my mother into letting Logan drive me home from church.

"Skyla, this is my Uncle Barron, Gage's dad."

"Nice to meet you." I shake his hand. He has a warm glow about him. He's tall and shares the same stunning blue eyes as Gage.

"Come into the kitchen." He holds open a double door, which leads into a stark white room with a long metal tray in the center. I blink twice at it before I realize the covered lump is probably a body awaiting some sort of death prep, and the thought makes me sway on my heels.

"Chin up." His uncle pinches my cheek, hard. "Sorry, I'm short on smelling salts."

"No, it's OK." This is not a freaking kitchen. It's a place where no one should eat, ever.

"You have any other gifts?" He asks as he takes the vial from Logan.

It's hard to imagine that dark crimson liquid bubbling up at the top is what keeps me going. That it holds the secrets to my so-called life. That I produce it deep inside my bones—that everybody does—is nothing short of a miracle.

"Gifts?" He asks again.

"Um, no. I don't think so. Do you?" I direct the last part toward Logan.

"A few."

His uncle cuts in before he has the chance to elaborate.

"What you have Skyla, is a unique gift. It's the trademark of a special faction of Nephilim known as Celestra."

"Celestra." I try it out on my lips—it tickles as it rolls from my tongue.

"Most Nephilim around these parts are Levatio. Once in a while you roll the genetic dice and you get a win."

"A win?"

"Celestra is the highest order of earthbound angels." He nods. "They have the ability to rule and other amazing gifts that have left them the most loathed faction this side of the universe."

"Loathed as in hated?" I give Logan a look of discontent. I'm not liking the idea of being hated—and by angels? That sounds illegal on a spiritual level and wrong on just about every other.

"Yes," Barron continues, "they're also nearly extinct. Then there's the Countenance faction—we refer to them as the Counts for short. They cover the earth like vermin, demand money from everyone like the world owes it to them."

"Sounds like a twisted form of government." I try to make light of the situation.

"Oh, they have their claws in that, too," he assures. "They're everywhere."

"So why are the Celestra nearly extinct?"

He exchanges a somber glance with Logan.

"Because, my love," his uncle bears into me with his cobalt eyes, "the Counts have made it their mission to have them eradicated."

It takes a long trip around the outskirts of my mind to grasp any one of my racing thoughts let alone verbalize a semi-coherent response. "Do I have a mark on my head? Did they kill my dad? Your parents?" I direct that last question toward Logan.

"Yes," Barron answers, "mostly likely yes, and definitely yes." He looks mildly amused, peering at me from over his frameless spectacles. "Once Logan's parents produced a near pure Celestra, they couldn't let them breed anymore." He says it matter of fact as though it were a well-understood fact.

"And my dad?"

"He produced you. But there's also the chance he was killed for his standing. You mentioned your sister doesn't seem to have this?"

I shake my head. I'm pretty sure she doesn't. I've tested her on many occasions holding her hand while thinking the most outlandish things just trying to get a rise out of her. If she can hear me, and she's hiding the fact, she deserves an Oscar every year for the rest of her life.

"Perhaps the Counts don't know about you yet," Barron shrugs, "but they will. They have a strong sense of smell when it comes to these things. Don't be remiss, they will kill if they feel you're a threat."

"Well, I'm not a threat." I pump a short-lived smile.

"You might be." He tousles my hair before walking away.

"We don't always know who they are," Logan says.

We sit on a bench overlooking the cemetery. It's so calm and peaceful here. The sun stretches her beams over the rolling hills and sets her reflection on the grave markers, making them sparkle like a thousand shards of glass.

"Who else is Nephilim besides you and Gage?"

"I just know us," he whispers. "There are a few people my uncle's age. I only know this because they hold council meetings. Once in a while the meetings are on Paragon. When you reach the age of enlightenment, they graft you in—tell you all their secrets." He wiggles his fingers when he says it. "It's sort of the big reveal."

"Why this certain age? They don't trust us because we're young?"

"Ageist bastards," he laughs a little when he says it.

"So how old do you have to be to know everything?"

"Thirty."

"Shut up." I push into him with my shoulder. You may as well not know anything if you have to wait all the way until you're thirty. Thirty is practically on the verge of senility.

"I'm serious. Thirty. Most Celestra die by then. Don't worry, you and I will make it. I have a strong assurance of this."

"And how, pray tell, do you know?" I like where's he's going. Even if his goal is to comfort me, it feels as though a giant casket has been lifted off my chest.

"Because Gage told me. He knows things. That's his gift."

"When did he say this?" I give his hand a gentle squeeze.

"The day before I met you," it comes out in earnest.

A light breeze picks up, and the dreary afternoon is transformed into a perfect summer day. I couldn't think of a better place to be than sitting in a cemetery with my favorite angel right by my side.

"Me neither." He gives a sly smile.

Logan brushes his lips against mine, soft as a feather.

13

Drama Mama

As promised, I dig through box after box of the crap we've managed to hoard all these years. Honestly, I thought we threw so much stuff away before we left L.A. I didn't think we'd have anything left to unpack.

Piles of my elementary school art and Mia's preschool endeavors gone awry clutter up the boxes. Not one note from my father, not a lock of his hair, or his favorite tie. I wonder why my mother bothered keeping my sister and me—obligation, or fear of prison.

"You have any whites?" Mom breezes past me on the way to the laundry room, her arms laden down with Tads dirty socks and underwear.

"You ever regret turning into Tad's live-in maid?" I taunt as she passes.

"Don't start a war you're not willing to finish," my mother bleats. A few crashes and bangs later she reemerges, the sound of running water soothes the room from behind.

"I don't see any of Dad's stuff." There's a note of defeat in my voice. I really don't get why we need to erase someone just because they're dead. Even Logan wants his dead girlfriend's diary, which sucks in a big way, but that's for another day.

"It's in there somewhere." She pushes a broken wicker basket to the side with her foot and comes over to where I'm seated.

"I think I want to put together a scrapbook. You know, of all the good times we used to have."

"What good times?" Her eyes widen with curiosity, pale as stones.

I'm pretty sure she's not trying to get me riled up, although it's backfiring on her big time.

"Come on, Mom—you remember the good times." I don't let her hear my disappointment even though this blatant dumb blonde shit she's trying to pull is really pissing me off.

"I don't remember too many of those, just a lot of yelling—not enough money and too many bills to pay." She picks up a deck of playing cards and pulls them out of the sleeve. "Anything in particular you want to share with me?"

Not really. But I don't say that, I say, "All you remember about Daddy is yelling and not having money?" The sky outside the window darkens, the driving wind sends the branch of a eucalyptus scraping across the glass.

"It was hard for the two of us. We had you when we were both so young."

"So you're saying I'm the reason you and Dad had a rough go of it?" I struggle to keep it together.

"That's not what I'm saying." She digs her palms into her eyes full with regret. "What I'm trying to say is—oh heck, Skyla, I don't know. It was hard, and it was even harder when he died. Thank God for Tad because without him..."

I hop to my feet and take the stairs two by two. I'd rather sit alone in my bedroom with Chloe's ghost. Maybe she'll detail to me how Logan touched her, how it felt to have him wanting her. I'll take anything over my mother and her dissertation on how Tad saved the day.

He sure as hell didn't save mine.

I walk around my bedroom in a slow methodical circle, tapping the walls and saying her name as if daring her to appear.

My mother doesn't bother coming up to repair any damage that may have occurred during our impromptu verbal scrimmage. Seems our relationship is on the path to a steady deterioration, and neither of us really gives a shit.

"Where are you Chloe? Afraid Logan might like me just a little bit better?" I whisper the words into the wall as though it were a part of her. "I would have had him anyway." I'm not really into pissing off Chloe, but she's become a good surrogate for my mother at the moment.

A drowsy feeling overcomes me, and I stagger over to the bed—flop down and indulge in the blank world behind my eyelids.

It feels like I'm falling—it feels unnatural like I'm rotating through the air in a series of erratic circles. I'm falling through space and time and landing right smack into a dream.

Do you know who I am? A girl in skintight jeans and a hot pink tank top beckons me over. Her long dark curls extend past her hips, and her eyes glint out like twin orange sunsets. She's pretty in a scary, poltergeist from your nightmares, sort of way.

Chloe? I don't hide my enthusiasm. Everyone around me knew her, and now I get to meet her, see her with my own eyes.

It's me. She bleeds a necrotic smile. *Do you know why I came?* Her body stretches out another foot taller easy as pulling taffy.

So you can tell me how much you hate me? Honestly, it's all I can deduce. I'm not sure if my sarcasm is coming in clear. My voice stagnates like I'm talking from inside a fishbowl.

I don't hate you, she emits in a haunting river of vocal quivers. *I called you here because I need you.*

You can't have Logan. I don't mean for it to sound so cold or territorial.

I still have Logan where it counts. She says it serious.

I don't think I want to help you with anything. Don't come knocking around these eyelids anymore.

I will myself to wake up. It takes a bionic effort on my part to flutter my lids and open my eyes. I roll off the bed and land on the floor, my stomach writhing from nausea.

If she comes back I'll smoke her out of existence.

I don't know how, but I will.

14

Game Changer

Brielle once again manages to talk me into a mall crawl.

Outside the air is thick with humidity, heavy as a sopping wet towel. A thick sheath of clouds press in the heat and turn the island into one big sauna. It's strangulating suffering in this airless environment devoid of any sunlight.

It's an outdoor mall so we don't have mercy of air conditioning unless we step into the stores, and already we've seen everything there is—twice.

We sit out under a giant umbrella eating our shared ice cream, a double scoop of chocolate from a cup. A herd of small children run in and out of a fountain, watching the water shoot up out of tiny spouts that line the area labeled, *wet zone.*

There's something strange about this day that doesn't settle well with me. My skin feels like it's on fire, and it has nothing to do with the bizarre dark heat wave we're embroiled in. It feels odd—as though someone's watching me, following me. I scour the vicinity like a hawk, looking for people, animals, an errant shop worker who happens to be leering in my direction, but nothing.

"You're thoroughly paranoid, you know that?"

I've made the mistake of sharing my thoughts with Brielle.

"I don't know." I stage my body out like a siren waiting to draw someone in. "It's like an instinct. I just know someone's watching. You ever get that feeling?"

"No—besides, you're starting to creep me out. It's the same kinds of stuff Chloe was saying before..." She shrugs and takes another bite of her ice cream.

"Really? Then maybe they're back?"

"Don't say that," her voice sharpens. "Don't ever say that, Skyla. There is nobody around us. Trust me I've looked. My dad is a detective, it's in my blood to know these things."

I don't let Brielle see how shaken I am. It's as if each passing moment brings them closer. Their intent is anything but good, that much I know. I can't help but wonder if it's the Counts. Bitch squad maybe? Most likely the latter, or worse, Tad and my mother.

"Oh thank God." Brielle stands up and lunges into someone behind me.

It's Gage.

"Hey!" I'm thrilled to see him, partly because Logan is never far behind and partly because I suddenly feel well protected. No offense to Brielle, but I'm pretty sure she's worthless in that department.

"You're late for your shift." He pats her on the arm.

"Oh shit! I'm so sorry! We have to go." She darts around and gathers her things.

"Hang out for a minute," Gage says to me. "I can give you a ride."

"Sure." I watch as Brielle freaks out on her way toward the parking lot.

"Drive careful," I shout. "Is Logan here?" I revert my attention back to the ebony haired god seated before me. He's already helping himself to the ice cream. He looks up and gives a wry smile.

"I'm not good enough?"

Something about the way he says it melts the pit of my stomach.

"Of course you're good enough. It's just you're not Logan." I'm not sure that made things better.

Gage leans back, takes me in without an apology. He lets his eyes roam free over my person, up and down like a body-scan until I clear my throat.

"You always rude like that?" I ask.

"I'm not trying to be rude. Sorry." His dark hair nestles in curls toward the base of his neck. Gage Oliver has got to be the hottest guy on the planet, next to Logan, of course. It's like they suffer from some genetic deformity that took over and accidently created two perfect beings. "Heard my dad's looking into things for you."

"Yeah, I'm pretty excited. I've never thought about myself as an angel before. More like the opposite." Not really, but I don't have anything else to say. I take a huge bite off my spoon and fill my mouth with chocolate to prevent me from saying anything that might sound stupid.

"Well you're definitely an angel." He arches his brows at me. "I know."

"And you know this because?"

"It's my gift."

"Oh, Logan mentioned it," I whisper. "He said you told him we weren't going to die until a ripe old age."

"Yeah, well, don't go doing anything stupid like standing in front of a train. Just because you're going to live doesn't mean you can't do it as a vegetable." His features darken.

"Right." Mental note: Gage equals buzz kill.

"I know something else about you." He looks me over with a studious intent.

A bird whistles to his right, a large black beast, far too monstrous to be a crow.

"Oh, my God!" I press my hand into my chest in horror at the sight. It sits perched on the trashcan directly next to Gage. It's gargantuan and demonic and looks as if it accidentally flew in from some prehistoric time period. Its feathers are the exact same hue of Gage's hair, and its eyes are glued to him with great interest. "Make it go away." I cover my face with my hands as a horrible tremor of fear darts through me.

I look up in time to see Gage flick his finger lightly into the air with no real malfeasance behind it.

The giant bird races into the sky quick as a demon, streaks across the hemisphere like a black billow of smoke until it evaporates into the grey nothingness of the sky.

"You made it do that didn't you?" It was something more than your typical scatting of a bird. Something in the way Gage nonchalantly directed his finger in the air, told me so much more.

"I did." He slumps into his seat as if bored with the effort he's having to put in with me.

"So what is it that you know?" I try to sound disinterested but really I want to reach over and rattle out all his secrets.

"I know you're going to marry me someday." He doesn't bother with a smile or a laugh, or anything to indicate he might be teasing.

"Well, I'm not."

He pulls his cheek to the side almost apologetically. "You will."

15

Virtue

The next afternoon, Logan calls and says he wants to take me somewhere. Of course, I said pick me up in fifteen minutes without even asking where. I'd go to the landfill if he wanted to.

I stayed up far too late last night, still afraid to sleep in my room. No scary dreams, thank God, but my head throbs from a lack of a solid eight.

Logan's monster truck gets here a whole five minutes before he does by way of noise pollution. I wait at the bottom of the driveway, and wave to him as soon as he drifts out of the fog.

"Hey you," I say, climbing into the cab.

"I would have come around to help you."

"No worries." I clasp his fingers from across the seat. I go to put my foot on the last wrung of the mini ladder and slip straight to the bottom. Without realizing what's happening I'm floating through the air, rising effortlessly into the truck by way of his hand wrapped around my wrist. "How'd you do that?" I marvel, shutting the door and reaching for my seatbelt.

"It's a gift."

"You're like really strong." My heart beats erratic, swallowing up the extra oxygen my brain would have normally needed for me to say something a little more articulate. "Can I do that?"

"I don't know, can you?"

"I don't think so."

He pulls out onto the main road and we start in on our adventure. Trees whiz by in a viridian blur. The fog rakes by in distended billows, faster and faster until it looks like we're going back in time, or forward, it could go either way and on Paragon, and this wouldn't surprise me.

"Your gifts can grow," he says. "It's rare, but they can manifest with time. Don't let anyone tell you that you can't do something. It's poison every single time."

Logan takes me to one of the most beautiful natural wonders ever created by the hand of God, a set of waterfalls.

The Falls of Virtue are located in the dead center of the island. There's a mountainous incline we climb seemingly forever until we crest up above the fog. The air is unusually clear—far more pristine than anything I was ever used to back in L.A.

"Wow." Their sheer beauty steals my breath away. A rainbow shivers across the three sacred falls, and glows in the warm veil of sunlight as if to greet us. "It's..." There are no words.

The mountain in the center disappears to greater heights, enwreathed in a layer of clouds at the base. The fog lies just beneath our feet, creating a mystical aura that floats above the water.

"You have unicorns here too?"

"Not at this location. They prefer the higher elevations where it snows," he teases.

"So that's where the water comes from?"

"Year round."

I step out to the rim of the lake. The falls are loud, but not deafening like other waterfalls I've been to. It's a soft enchanting rush, a never-ending flow of constant beauty that fills the waiting pool beneath. The water holds the same cobalt hue as Gage's eyes, and for a minute he sears through my mind as if he's admonishing me. Truth is—I'm still trying to digest those last few words he spoke.

"This is where I want to get married someday." Not to Gage. Maybe it's not the thing to say to the guy who's not quite officially your boyfriend, but it feels right. This place practically warrants profound statements about ones future. Before Logan gets too bogged down with regret over bringing me here, I offer, "Gage said I was going to marry him." I roll my eyes at the absurdity.

Logan's smile drops from his face like a stone. His eyes widen and he looks right through me, dazed.

"So it must be true," he says.

"I'm not marrying Gage," I say, flatly. "I thought it was funny. Brielle thinks maybe he has a crush on me."

"He does." He's still gazing out into nowhere, right through my skull.

"Anyway, I'm not into him," I pause trying to wake him from his stupor with a wave of my hand, "I'm into you."

He snaps out of his trance and his lips pick up a slight curve.

"I'm into *you*." He comes in soft with a string of silent kisses, then heads into something deeper we can both bite into.

I love kissing Logan. Kissing Logan at the Falls of Virtue is like stepping into a fairytale. Suddenly I'm transported to a land with dragons and villains. Of course, I'm the princess, which in turn makes Logan the perfect prince.

He pulls back, bouncing one soft kiss off the tip of my nose.

"You up for a swim, princess?"

"I don't have my bathing suit." I give a wry smile. I hate when I forget he can hear me, and I have a feeling I know what's coming.

"Swim in your underwear, or without. Your choice."

"I don't have a towel." It races out of me. Besides, I'm not sure if I'm up for the big fleshy reveal.

"I have a few in the truck for emergencies."

"Does this qualify as an emergency?"

"It's the only one I know of." His face fills with devilish intent. "I'll stay in my boxers." He holds up his hand like a boy scout.

The thought of Logan stripping down to his skivvies makes me weak—makes me writhe inside intense with pleasure. This can't be good. Nothing good is going to come of this, I can feel it.

"Sure." I walk around the truck and take off my sweater. I happen to have on my bright pink bra with the rhinestone jewel inset in the middle, which practically demands to be seen.

I go to peel off my jeans, and for the life of me I can't remember what underwear I'm wearing.

Oh please, God, don't let them be white mamas. I have my fair share of granny panties no thanks to my mom's desire to keep me amply supplied, and once in a while I'll put them on. If that's today I'm going to have to seriously reconsider this whole idea. I tug past my hips only to reveal with great delight a pair of yellow lace boy shorts, which is great because they cover a multitude of shaving issues.

A light tap ripples across the hood of the truck.

I traipse back around and find Logan standing there in all his celestial glory, plus boxers.

Heat rushes to my face as I feel him take me in. Per square inch I'm wearing the exact amount of clothing I've worn a million times before to the beach—technically more if you count the G-string my mother has no clue about.

He takes my hand and pulls me into a careful kiss. I can feel the warmth of his body—his bare skin against mine. It feels sinful and perfectly right at the very same time.

"You think the water's cold?" I say pushing him back gently before things go too far.

"I hope so."

We hold hands and dive in together off a small ledge near the center of the lake. The icy bite of the water feels like it has the ability to skin me alive. We might as well be swimming in arctic springs it's so freaking cold. My skin goes numb from the shock of it—feels thick as a rubber wetsuit.

Logan and I dive under each of the three falls, stealing secret kisses that seem to last an eternity beneath each one.

There's no way I would ever become Gage's anything. Logan has me totally and completely. This is something that surpasses the length of years, the ladder of time. We're building something eternal. I can feel it.

Something dark glints to my right, a shadow of something moving in the evergreen, then I see it.

The raven.

All afternoon I wonder what it means.

16

Mixed

It rains the entire next day. Brielle finishes up her shift at six and invites Drake and me down to the bowling alley to play a few rounds.

After paying for shoes and two games, I'm drained of nearly every penny of my Christmas money from last year.

"I'll give you a refund if you want." Logan has already offered to give back my money, twice.

"I'm not here to rob you." Although, I'm not above taking advantage of him in other ways. A naughty smile glides across my face.

"No, but it's my job to rob *you*, and I don't feel too good about it." He presses an assortment of buttons, and the register springs open.

"How about you take me to dinner and a movie? We'll call it even."

"Deal." He slams the register shut, and I get out of line, so he can help the people behind me.

It's busy tonight, like everyone on the island decided it was a good night to bowl.

I see Brielle waving us over in the far corner of the room. Drake strides ahead, as if she's waving at him exclusively, and judging by the come hither look in her eyes, the cleavage down to her navel, she just might be.

"Hey, you playing?" Gage flicks at the shoes in my hands.

His hair is slicked back, exposing the sheer perfection of his features. I'm shocked there aren't a hundred girls mobbing him at any given time. Logan's looking pretty hot too, but I would never want to imagine a single girl mobbing him, let alone a hundred.

"You always this bright?" I can't help responding to the natural inclination I have to be a little mean to Gage. I'm afraid if I give him the wrong signals he'll think the wedding is on, and he might send his pet bird after me again.

"I'm off in ten. If you want to make it even, I can hang out."

"Whatever." I look back at Logan. The line just exploded out the door. Wish he were off in ten.

Drake sets up the computer. Instead of Drake, he actually writes *Count Drakeula* and I want to crawl in a hole. For Brielle he writes *sexy thang*—again displaying his incredible lack of judgment. Thankfully for me, he just puts Skyla. Gage hops over before he's done filling in the queue, so his name goes beneath mine.

"You think it'll look like that on our wedding invitations?" I tease, leaning over to put on my shoes.

He folds his arms and slides deep in his seat. He doesn't find any humor in the situation, just chews the inside of his cheek out of frustration.

I miss both Brielle and Drake's turns because I'm too busy staring down Gage— trying to decode his mysterious aura.

"You're up." He kicks playfully at my foot.

I'm sharing a hot pink eight-pound ball with Brielle. Before I head down the lane to shoot I note she scored a strike, so it's got to be good luck. I take a running start then go to release, only it doesn't release, it sticks to my fingers popping off in midair and lands hard as an anvil on the gleaming wood floors. Sounds like a cannon just went off.

My shoulders pinch up around my neck, and I'm praying no one saw, only I know Gage did for sure because I can feel him burning a hole through my shirt right this very second.

I turn to find not only Gage, but an equally stunned Brielle and Drake gawking at me as though I had just committed the most heinous sporting crime ever. And to my delight and horror the bitch squad happens to be picking out balls with none other than Logan just past our table—they're all probably wondering who gave the blonde jackass a bowling ball to play with.

The return cycle spits out the hot pink nightmare, and I pick it up again. Logan appears next to me holding a blue marbled ball that looks as though he's shrunk down the earth and sky for me.

"Try this one, it might be a better fit." He takes the monster ball with a serious mind of its own away from me. I'm surprised he doesn't come after me for damages.

"Thanks."

"Here, I'll show you how to shoot." He walks me down the beginning of the lane and bends my arm back. I can feel his leg press in hard against mine. His arm slips just behind my elbow, his warm neck cradles in the crook of my shoulder.

I never knew bowling could be such an erotic sport.

"Neither did I," he whispers hot in my ear.

I laugh as we chuck the ball awkwardly down the lane. Only this time it's not an automatic gutter ball. This time, it rolls all the way down and knocks back half the pins.

Logan and I exchange high-fives.

I hop back to my seat filled with glee, even though Logan went back to answer some ludicrous question Michelle screeched over at him. I watch as he sits down at their table and starts filling in their computer board.

Gage bullets his ball down the lane with a vengeance and gets a strike right off the bat. I'd accuse him of dumb luck, but he's probably bowled in the dark and achieved the same feat.

I glance over my shoulder and catch Logan's name popping up on the neighboring screen.

"I thought he was working tonight," I muse to Gage as he takes a seat.

"He's the boss. Always doing what he likes." He stretches his arm across the back of the curved bench, his fingers touching the top of my shoulder.

Brielle screams and shouts with great exuberance from her second strike in a row, which I missed again—some friend I am.

"Congratulations," I say without the required enthusiasm.

"Is that what's bugging you?" She clicks her tongue over at the next table. "Logan has a way of getting around." She pulls a face. "Sorry. He's just friendly that way."

"Is this true?" I ask Gage below a whisper.

"I try not to affiliate myself with rumors," there's a palpable sarcasm in his tone. "Judge for yourself."

I try to look back without being so obvious. Logan has his hand on Michelle's arm as she leans in and whispers something to him. I know what he's doing. He's reading her mind. I'm sure it's loaded with equal portions of lust and lunacy.

Logan looks back and sees me watching. He gives a brief wink, a barely there expression of acknowledgement, before turning his full attention to whatever it is she's filling his head with.

They openly share a laugh.

If I didn't know any better, I'd swear they were a couple.

17

Snake

The sky has split open. It yawns long stretches of rain—torrential downpours— until the roadways look like muddy rivers polluted with battery acid, mud the color of rust rising up on its sides.

Brielle called and asked if Drake and I wanted to come over, hang out and watch a movie, so we go.

The house looks different. More structured, less carefree than the last time I was here. It's been dusted and swept and the dishes are not migrating all over the counter, most likely courtesy of Brielle herself.

She's wearing a brand new black sweater with peek-a-boo lace trim. It's embarrassingly apparent she's not wearing a bra. Deductive logic reasons this by the way she's bouncing around. Her face is done up kabuki style with too much makeup and not enough reality left for the discriminating eye. Something tells me I'll be watching this movie on her larger than life plasma all by my lonesome.

"So Drake," she over annunciates his name, "would you like a tour of the house?"

"Really?" I ignore the opening credits and turn down the volume. "Is that where this is headed? Because I could leave, and you two can tour the world for all I care."

"No, no! Don't do that, please." Brielle purses her lower lip in a dramatic fashion.

"Fine I'll stay."

As soon as they head upstairs, I pluck out my phone and start texting Logan.

Where are you? I'm doing time at B's. She's getting busy with monkey boy. ~S

A fair amount of the movie goes by before my cell vibrates over the coffee table.

Work. Want to come? I can use the help. Must be a great day to bowl. What is B doing with a monkey?

I hear the distinct knock of a headboard whack against the wall a few times then nothing. I'm afraid to move, or breathe, and I want nothing more than to run home in the pouring rain and pull the covers up over my head. I'm not sure that I'm fit to live in a world where monkey boy gets action with a beautiful girl like Bree, especially not if said action is taking place right above my head. It feels like an unholy violation listening to it in real time.

Trust me, I'd much rather help u. It is the perfect day for bowling. And to answer your question, rutting. ~S

It takes less than a minute for him to respond.

Rutting?! You have a way with words. You should write poetry.

I laugh at the thought. If I wrote poetry it wouldn't be about my rodent-like stepbrother and newfound best friend. I would pen rivers of sappy words, all strung together in an effort to capture the intense feelings I have for Logan. I might just do that anyway.

I'll save my poems for you. I promise they will not include the word rutting. Ever. ~S

I try and formulate a poem for him in my mind, but each time the word love pops up uninvited. Is this what it feels like to be in love? What I feel for Logan?

He buzzes right back.

Rutting is my new favorite word. BTW, Gage wants me to give you a message. He very much looks forward to rutting with you.

Ha. Ha.

Tell Gage anytime. I'm waiting and coincidentally very lonely at this very moment. ~S

Less than ten seconds.

Never mind. I suddenly have a great disdain for the word rutting. You must never rut with Gage. Promise me this.

My heart warms at his sudden burst of jealousy.

Will you rut with others? Turnabout is fair play. ~S

No.

Promise. ~S

I place down the phone and settle in to watch the rest of the movie. It was a strange yet comforting conversation with Logan. I think I'm one inch away from being his girlfriend. I wonder how it gets to be official. Write on your Facebook wall? Change your status to read *in a relationship*? Or maybe it just becomes so painfully obvious that after a while everybody and their mother knows. I've never had a boyfriend before, but I'd sure love the answer to these questions.

18

Take Down

It's not fifteen minutes into cheer practice that I manage to tweak my ankle entirely on my own. I'd love to blame just about anybody for today's literal misstep, but the bulk of the blame is on me—OK—all of it.

"How'd you do this?" Logan's football coach hovers over me. He presses his finger down over the growing bulge until I squeal in pain.

"Nice method of evaluation," I slap his hand away, "if this were the middle-ages."

His eyes bug out with surprise. I don't really care what he thinks, I'm not one of his jocks who needs to take whatever he dishes, especially if what he's dishing involves pain.

"Ice it. Stay off it for a day or two. Nothing's broken." He rises to his feet then claps his hands extra loud in an effort to break up the crowd.

Logan reaches down and picks me up effortlessly with one arm under both knees, the other supporting my back. "Where to?"

"I need ice." I try not to let on that I'm on the verge of tears. It's not so much the pain than the embarrassment and extra attention. I was never a big fan of either.

"I know just the place."

Brielle walks beside us over to his truck.

"There's no way you'll get her in there," she says, full with concern over the aerial feat Logan is ready to attempt.

He has Gage hold open the door and block Brielle's view as he lifts me safe into the seat as though I were as heavy as a hollowed out egg.

Gage hops in the back and we take off.

"First sunny day in a week and I blow it."

"Blaming yourself for an injury is a defeatist attitude," Logan says, looking at the road. "It's time to relax and let your body heal."

"Wise and true." I wave to Gage out the back window.

We turn left instead of right at the light, away from the bowling alley or my house, so I'm clueless as to where he might be taking me.

"Falls of Virtue?" Actually that's to the left as well. It's just my round about way of grilling him for details.

"Nope. I know somewhere with much stronger healing properties. The foods pretty good too."

"If there's an ER involved, count me out. I hate hospitals almost as much as I hate blood." A quick spike of panic shoots through me at the possibility.

"No ER, I promise."

"Is there rutting involved?"

"Only if you want there to be."

I wince as I shift my weight.

"There's a yellow lab named Charlie," he starts, "some hot chocolate, a grilled cheese sandwich, and an ice pack involved— maybe some reality TV."

"Sounds like Heaven."

"Almost is."

A black sports car with deep tinted windows swings over into our lane and just keeps coming. It races toward us without wavering.

"Do something," I scream in a panic.

The left lane is clogged with traffic and there's a steep embankment to our right.

I can't look. I go to cover my eyes, but as I do I notice the cars alongside us are no longer racing in the other direction, the people in them frozen in horror as they observe what's about to happen.

The truck however is still moving, flying in slow motion over the oncoming traffic as we pass it—obnoxiously slow. Logan takes out his phone and snaps a picture of the men in the vehicle.

Then the world speeds up again, and we're traveling at a normal velocity on the open stretch of road ahead as if nothing happened at all.

I look over at the truck bed and catch Gage hopping back inside, settling in.

It was him—Gage. He carried us over. Super human strength must be their shared gift.

I wonder what else they can do.

Logan and Gage run theories past each other of who those men could have been.

"There's a meeting at Nicholas Haver's in two days," Gage informs him.

"We're there." They share a fist bump in the kitchen of their palatial home. Their parents aren't home and I'm sort of disappointed. I've met the uncle, but I'm dying to meet Logan's aunt, my supposed future mother-in-law. I guess she'd be my mother-in-law either way. I don't know why, but I'm fascinated with other people's mothers.

"I want to go," I interject.

"Go where?" Logan's busy pulling out the ingredients for our lunch.

"The meeting. It's a Celestra thing, right?"

"Faction council. You're a Celestra," Gage corrects.

"There's no way you can go." Logan plucks a pan from underneath the cabinet. "You could endanger yourself. The less people know you have Celestra blood, the better."

"Once you're on their radar..." Gage and Logan share a look of discontent.

"Once I'm on their radar, they'll want me dead."

"Not necessarily right away. They might give you a fighting chance." Gage folds his arms across his chest.

"Like you?" I direct it over at Logan.

"Apparently, I have more than a fighting chance. I'm going to live to a ripe old age, remember?" He darts a look over to Gage.

"We both are," I confirm.

"Remember what I said about vegetables." Gage slaps his hand against the doorframe on the way out of the kitchen.

I'm going to that meeting, neither Logan or Gage can stop me.

I watch as Logan fires up the stove, sprays the pan with oil.

It will all work out in the end because I'm going to live to be a ripe old age.

A bitter acid rises to the back of my throat.

Live to be a ripe old age.

Gage says so.

If I follow that logic...then I must also believe I'm going to marry him, which I don't.

Do I?

19

Scheme

"Wake up!" My mother tears open the curtains. "Rise and shine and give God your glory, glory!" Her voice grates in my ears. I think I would have appreciated bamboo shoots beneath my fingernails just a little bit more. Her singing solidifies my perpetual bad mood for the day.

A dapple of pale sunlight streaks across my lids as I roll over, trying to ignore both it and the happy gale force hurricane disguised as my mother.

"Come on, Skyla." She rattles me by the shoulder. "Tad and I have a surprise for you—for the whole family. Come on."

My mother evacuates the premises taking her fanatical jubilation with her, and the room reverts back to the peace and calm I've come to appreciate. I try to absorb the tranquility, the lull in the air, in an effort to balance out the agitation she just drilled into my bones.

I get up on my elbow and peer out the window. Fog softens the harshness of reality, steals the definition from the world— blankets itself around everything as if it were some supernatural form of protection. I've come to love Paragon—its moody days, cool star-filled nights, the falls, even the cemetery is a thing of beauty. Most of all, I love the people. It's amazing how connected I feel in just a short period of time. It's like I've always belonged here, like everything else was just a waypoint until I arrived at my final destination.

A hard knock detonates on the other side of the door.

"*Now*, Skyla," Tad barks.

I swing my legs over the edge of the bed and push into my flip-flops before heading downstairs.

My mother has her hair done, her good jeans on, make-up in place, and it's not quite seven-thirty.

A small sprig of hope rises in me at the thought of this being their big divorce announcement. Now that would be a surprise. That's one family meeting I'm very much anticipating.

I plop down on the couch next to Mia and Melissa, while Drake busies himself by pouring a box of cereal down his throat.

"Your father and I—" my mother starts.

Tad cuts her off with a brief wave. She nods submissively and holds out her hands as if to say take it away.

I hate how he does that to her. It's not the first time he's interrupted when she's about to say something. It's like he thinks whatever's about to come out of his mouth is far more important.

"It's sort of my baby," he says before continuing. "Althorpe has set up a meeting for me in Seattle tomorrow, and I thought what better way to get to know the surrounding area than taking a train ride through the local mountains? So, your mother and I," he drapes his arms over her shoulder, "we've decided that it's going to be our first official family get away."

"A train?" Mia squeals into Melissa's face as if Santa himself were going to be on it.

"Cool." Drake pours the remainder of milk into his bowl without missing a beat.

"Have fun." The thought of having the house to myself for the weekend sounds more than delicious.

"We will have fun—with you." My mother chides. "This is non-negotiable."

"If she's not going I'm not going," Drake says with a full mouth.

"Oh no, he's definitely going. I'm not staying in the house alone with him." I'm sure he'll have Brielle over the second they hit the bottom of the driveway. I'm not interested in bearing witness to another fuck-fest.

"You're both going," Tad bellows. "Everybody get ready. We want to try and make the afternoon ferry." He gathers his briefcase off the kitchen counter and heads upstairs.

"I'm not going," I say, looking dead on at my mother. If she really wants a challenge I'll give her one.

"Why, Skyla? Why?" She doesn't bother hiding her exasperation.

Mia and Melissa amble upstairs in a frenzy of excitement.

"Because..." I pause considering my options. "I'm on my period." I give a sly smile over to Drake while my mother goes over and busies herself in the kitchen. "Monster, debilitating cramps," I groan, clutching at my abdomen.

"Gross." Drake does a magnificent disappearing act.

"Do you really have monster cramps?" She stops short of scrubbing the granite counter raw.

"Yes." I absolutely hate lying with a passion, but if it means getting me off of a seventy-two hour detail with the step monkey—where I would be confined in a glorified casket as we gawk at landscape, I'll do it.

"I'd be napping the whole time and..." Tad walks by in the middle of my spiel. "If I'm sleeping in a drug induced coma I can't appreciate the scenery, and you'll be wasting all that money on the ferry, not to mention food and lodging."

Tad's ears pull back so far he looks like a rat.

"You can stay." He continues to the kitchen.

"What do you mean, she can stay?" Mom objects.

"She's right. She can sleep here for free. It saves us at least a hundred dollars, and face it, we need that hundred dollars." His posture straightens as he says it.

Chalk one up for me. I'll keep his tight-wad ways in mind more often.

Tad walks back down the hall leaving my mother to penetrate me freely with her hostile lasers.

"You win," she says without emotion. "But don't think you're any less a member of this family." She strides past me in a fury, her jeans scissoring up against each other with a loud swish.

I won.

I'll be at that faction meeting tomorrow night, and nobody can stop me.

20

Dream

It takes a small eternity for Tad and Mom to organize the troops, or what's left of them. By the time the girls and Drake shower they've already missed the first ferry, so I have to remain doubled over on the couch a lot longer than anticipated. My mother makes sure I take a pain pill under her watchful supervision because God forbid I should be left alone with a bottle of glorified Aspirin, and yet they don't lock up the liquor. It doesn't matter. I don't drink—hate the flavor—hate the feeling.

By the time I bolt the door behind them I'm feeling genuinely sleepy so I head on up to my room and crash.

Chloe comes to me in a dream. It's that *oh crap* moment when you realize the dream you're having, the one that started out perfectly normal, has morphed into a nightmare and now all you want is to do is claw out of it like a cat at the bottom of a hopelessly deep well.

Skyla. She calls to me down a very long hall. It's dark, save for the light emanating from an open door. I can see the frame of a woman, dark hair flowing like tendrils. I know it's her. I can feel it, feel *her.*

What do you want? I cry out. This is no vague panic gripping me. There is a very real danger here. My heart jumps in my throat, vibrating tenaciously like a fish out of water. This must be what it feels like to die.

You have enemies, Skyla. I didn't think I had them, but I was warned and didn't listen. If you're not careful there's a shallow grave that waits for you.

That's not what Gage said. It's funny how now, in my dream, I've accepted him as the final authority over my future.

I said the grave waited for you. I never said you'd be in it. They want to watch you bleed. She holds out her arm exposing long precision cut gashes. *They ran all kinds of experiments on me. They kept my body down there for twelve days. They could keep you a lifetime. They're not interested in your pain, Skyla. You need to stay away from the Faction Council. And most of all steer clear of Logan. Your life depends on it. Or else everything you know will change. And you'll spend the rest of your life running.*

Don't come to me again. I tremble holding onto the wall. It quivers with me. I can feel the vibration trailing up my shoulder.

If that's what you wish. Chloe evaporates into nothing more than a smoky film.

I bolt up out of bed in a sweat, my shirt clinging to me cold as ice.

Why would she want me to steer clear of Logan? She can't still want him for herself—she's dead. Someone needs to refresh the rules of a successful relationship with her. Then again, if I loved Logan and lost him, I wouldn't be above haunting his new girlfriend. What's a little nightmare, now and then?

Since I'm alone for the very first time ever—I do what any other red-blooded American girl would do, invite my boyfriend over.

I clean for the next several hours. I had no idea what a freaking mess Mia and Melissa were capable of. They've got clothes behind the sofa, under the cushions, a trail of trash that snakes around the entire house, and the downstairs bathroom looks like a cosmetics factory exploded. And by the way, why aren't Mom and Tad all over their asses for the carnage they've create?

A gentle knock emanates from the door. I smooth down the lace top I borrowed from Brielle last week. I try to push the fact it's the same top she wore on her sexcapade with Drake out of my mind, but unlike her I'm wearing a bra and not planning on stripping off the first chance I get, or the second.

"Hi!" I motion for him to come inside.

Logan is resplendent. He looks polished as a male model. He's wearing a soft cologne that smells woodsy and sweet like the leaves from a juniper. I can't resist wrapping my arms around him and landing a soft kiss over his lips. Something warms my chest, so I pull back a bit. He's holding a white paper bag that smells like Italian food.

"Dinner." He holds it up triumphantly.

I turn on the TV and we sit side by side in the family room eating our eggplant sandwiches.

"So I had this freaky dream." A huff of laughter escapes my chest to let him know I totally don't believe in stuff like that.

"Tell me all about it." He sets down his plate and knocks back the rest of his soda.

"It was about Chloe." I put it out there.

He straightens his back against the cushion.

"It was stupid," I offer.

"She say something to you?"

I wonder if he wants to hear some weepy romantic proclamation—to know that she's still pining for him on the other side.

"I don't really want to talk about it."

"If she has a message, I'd like to know what it is." He caresses my hand, clasps our fingers tight.

"I know what you're doing."

Then tell me.

"She doesn't think I should go to the council meeting tomorrow night."

And you won't. Logan looks certain, but more than that, like he won't allow it.

"I have a right to be there. Besides she ended it with all this psychobabble about me steering clear of you. Are you happy? She's trying to meddle in our relationship from the great beyond."

"Relationship?" The curve of a smile erases the worry from his forehead.

Oh God, I used the R word—and to a guy. Next thing you know I'll be telling him he's my boyfriend.

I'll take that title. He pulls me up over to his lap. *No council meeting. Promise?*

"Promise." I force myself to clear my mind of any unnecessary clutter. Why waste precious time with my new boyfriend when the meeting is an entire twenty-four hours away?

21

Unrest

It's ten after midnight and Logan is pressing me to let him sleep on the downstairs couch.

"No."

"Why not? Won't you sleep better knowing I'm down here to protect you?"

"No. I'll want to be down here, doing this," I squeeze my arms tight around his waist. "Then neither of us will get a good night's rest. Plus I'll have to lie to my mother again when she asks if any boys stayed over. I've met my quota on lying for the month."

"That's noble," he says without enthusiasm. He gets up off the couch slowly, helping me up in the process. "I open tomorrow." He presses out a smile. "If you start dying of boredom you're welcome to join me."

"Gee thanks." I tilt my head to the side in an effort to emphasize my sarcasm. I hadn't really thought about a job yet. I guess I need to see what kind of load I'm stuck with next semester. I'd hate to be doing my homework on the job.

"The job's yours if you want it, and I'll let you get away with doing your homework on the side."

"It creeps me out when you do that."

"Only because you keep forgetting. I'm not trying to pry. It's just out there—loud as speaking."

"You're right. So, anyway, when will I see you?"

"After my shift I have a two hour window before Gage and I head out to the meeting. What are you going to be up to?"

"Just hanging out with Bree. Come over before you leave."

"You got it."

We stand in the doorframe of the moonless night savoring our goodnight kiss. The cool night air breezes past us, circling my bare ankles with its arctic chill.

Logan heads down the porch on the way to his truck.

"Remember, I'm just a phone call away," he says before hopping inside.

I watch as he backs out of the driveway and disappears down the street.

I don't remember the last time I was alone in a house by myself. It's one of those things that rarely happens with a busy family like ours. For sure I've never been alone at this house. Come to think of it, I've never spent the night alone at any house, ever.

A shiver runs through me as I shut and bolt the door. I'd turn on the heater if I knew how to work it, so much for it being August.

The hollow of my footsteps echoes off the walls as I make my way back to the family room. I switch the TV off, and the house fills with a deafening silence. It sounds less than natural so I switch it back on and turn down the volume. I'll leave it on for the night. It'll make it look like someone's home, sort of like a safety mechanism. No one in their right mind will want to break in if they think someone's wide-awake downstairs. Then again, criminals are rarely in their right mind.

I peer out the window over in the direction of Bree's house. An entire thicket of overgrown pines, barricades my view. It's not important. It's not like seeing a light on over there would have made me feel safer.

I head up to my bedroom, leaving on all the downstairs lights. Tad will probably have a heart attack when he sees the electric bill, so at least some good will come from this.

It's strange how everything looks different, *sounds* different when there's nobody in the house but you.

I head into my bathroom to brush my teeth. I'm far too lazy to take off my makeup or change into my PJ's. Besides, jeans and a sexy shirt will totally come in handy when I run out the front door screaming.

A dark figure appears from behind, and I jump, holding out my toothbrush like it's some diabolical weapon someone might actually fear.

"Who's there?" I spit the foam out of my mouth and wipe the excess off my lips with a towel.

I felt someone there behind me, *felt* them.

A loud thump emanates from downstairs, which sends me immediately searching my jeans for my cell.

"Shit!" I panic. I distinctly remember leaving it in the kitchen next to the sink, which happens to be the most distal point from where I'm standing. And thanks to Tad's superhuman tightwad capabilities there is no landline in this freaking house!

A sharp rasping sound rubs against my window and sends me sailing downstairs in a dramatic screaming tirade.

My heart attempts to jackhammer out of my chest as I speed over to my phone, but it's gone.

"Skyla?" My name echoes from behind.

I freeze.

In my entire life I have only peed my pants once. I was in the fifth grade, and Laura Henderson, my then best friend, had me laughing so hard I released a small river of urine going down the steps of where we were seated during lunch. I'll never forget that feeling, watching helpless as the concrete darkened around me, my shame spreading along with it.

I turn slow toward the glass back door that leads to a tiny porch. I've yet to visit the back of the house, and for all I know there could be an entire cemetery out there.

A woman with shaggy hair waves at me. Her erratic smile is far too enthusiastic for my liking. I can't make out her body just the paper white skin of her face. She jumps and her eyes shut tight, her tongue bulging out of her mouth. A brown shredded rope cinches around her neck. It goes straight up past the door, and she starts in on a slow spin as her hair flattens against the glass.

A violent series of screams sail from my vocal cords.

I spot my phone on the table and run to the closet and call Brielle.

22

Party

The light from the crack in the curtains tickles me until I shove a pillow over my face and try to continue with the pleasant dream-deprived coma I was experiencing.

The volume on the TV rises, and I peek from under the pillow to find Brielle munching on a bag of chips with her hair disheveled and mascara smudged down to her cheek.

"Crazy night," I say, forcing myself to sit up. "Thanks for coming."

As soon as Brielle got here we went straight to the back door to find a bushy red branch had fallen off one of the trees. It must have been an illusion. I was so tired. It couldn't have been real. Could it?

"I've sent a mass text out, so we should have a ton of people," she says, playing with her phone.

"A ton of people?" A part of me is still asleep.

"At the party. You have anything we could put out for food? Or never mind, I told them nine o'clock so everyone should have eaten by then. My mom has these cool wireless speakers I'll bring over and hook it up to my iPod. There's a—"

"Stop. I'm not having a party. You can mass text everyone back and let them know it's been canceled."

"I can't do that. Besides, school starts in a few weeks. Doesn't your mom want you to meet everybody?" She gives a sly grin. "Killing two birds with one stone."

"She does." And doesn't Logan want me busy tonight so I can't sneak off to the council meeting? "I guess we're going to have a party."

And I'm going to kill two birds with one stone.

Brielle hauls the speakers over, and before I realize it, I'm enjoying the music exploding throughout the house.

Brielle suggests we leave the lights off and open all the curtains, but it's pitch black both inside and out, so I pull a bunch of camping lanterns from the garage and set them out all over.

"Everything looks so cool!" I hold both of Logan's hands and jump up and down like an idiot in an effort to look convincing. Then I drop them like he's got the plague and head over to the front door securing it open for the onslaught. A few kids are already hanging out on the porch, and according to Bree tons more are on the way. I need Logan to believe I'm not going anywhere tonight, that this party is my pet project and that I want nothing more than to oversee the whole thing, which I sort of do. Lousy night to have a faction meeting, if you ask me.

"So maybe after the meeting, Gage and I will drop by again." Logan comes over and wraps his arm around my shoulder. As long as he's not touching my flesh, I don't have to work so hard on blanking out my mind.

A crowd wanders in and soon the downstairs fills in with bodies.

"So how come Brielle spent the night?"

"I got scared." I pull a face. I don't tell him about the woman dangling from a rope out the backdoor. I may be headed for the loony bin, but I don't need to let the entire world in on my journey.

"You should have called me." He pushes into me gently, landing my back flat against the wall. His lips press against mine, and I try to enjoy his wonderful deep kisses while creating a force field of white noise within my mind.

He pulls back and gives a curious look.

"What? I can't enjoy the fruit of your lips?"

His eyes twitch around the room as though he senses something.

"What's wrong?" His expression has me worried. Maybe he detects something or someone left over from the night before.

"What happened last night?"

"Nothing. A branch fell down and hit the window. I freaked out."

"There's something else." He walks through the river of bodies and down to the kitchen. His head turns slowly toward the back door, and his eyes widen with surprise.

I hide behind his shoulder and peer out carefully. The last thing I want to do is scream like a maniac in front of the entire student body of West Paragon High.

It's Michelle. The door's wide open, and Michelle's sitting there smoking a cigarette flanked by Emily and Lexy, creating a disgusting cloud of bitchiness.

Logan's chest rumbles against me as though he were going to say something, but doesn't.

"What did you think you were going to see?" I ask in a hushed tone.

"Something evil," he whispers back.

"Looks like you were right."

"Looks like I was." He trembles with an inaudible laugh. "I didn't want to tell you this last night, but Chloe thought this place was haunted."

I take in a sharp breath. That explains more than a few things.

"I can spend the night if you like," he offers.

His offer is a balm to my newfound misery, although I question if he's telling the truth or utilizing scare tactics to his advantage.

"That's OK. I have Bree."

"I'll stop by after the meeting anyway." *Besides, there's something I want to show you that you may not have discovered about the house.*

"That it grows eight furry legs at night, and it's really a tarantula?"

His brows knit together.

Gage pops up behind him and slaps him on the shoulder. "Time."

"All right." He takes me by the hand and we move swiftly toward the front. "Expect me after midnight."

He drops a kiss on my forehead and disappears into the crowd.

I'll be seeing you long before then, I muse. *Only you won't know it.*

23

Awakening

I found Nicholas Haver's address this afternoon in a Paragon Island phonebook at the foot of Tad's desk. I thought I'd have to dig for hours, scan the Internet, pick Brielle's mom for information, but it was all so easy.

I head upstairs and change from my jeans to a charcoal running suit. I want to make every effort to blend into the night. Really I'm only planning on hanging out on the periphery to get a feel of what's going on—eaves drop if I'm lucky. Besides, didn't Logan say you needed to be thirty to go to one of these? Or maybe you needed to be thirty to learn all of the benefits? Who the hell cares. All I know is if Logan and Gage think they can go—so do I.

"Hey." Brielle grabs me by the arm as I dig out the spare key to the minivan from the kitchen. Lucky for me Tad would rather pay a cab than risk his precious ten-year old body wagon get stolen from the pier. Little did he know I would be the one stealing it—borrowing it. "Isn't this great?" She bounces into me.

Ellis Harrison shadows her from behind. I remember him from the party he threw when I first got here. He's tall, good looking and his teeth glow in the dark. I don't know why Brielle doesn't go for him instead of Drake—so many choices to make and such poor choices being made.

"I gotta make a food run. I'm starving."

"Are you kidding?" Clearly she wasn't expecting me to leave my own party.

"No really. I'll get a ton of food and be right back."

"You can't feed all these people!"

Something in the living room breaks, sounds like glass, and I'm praying it's not a window.

We head over to find a bottle exploded all over the floor.

"I'll get some towels." Brielle offers rushing back to the kitchen.

I ditch out the front, the cold night air penetrates right through my clothes with a glacial chill, making me wish I'd brought a jacket.

"I'll go with you."

I don't even notice Ellis at my heels until I unlock the minivan, and he piles in.

"You can't come." I shoo him out with my fingers as I start the engine. Technically I don't have my driver's license. I was way too petrified to drive around L.A. so I took my sweet time getting my learners permit. Plus, it probably didn't help that my father died in a fiery freeway collision right about the same time. Nothing to dampen your zest for driving like a little vehicular homicide.

"I want to." He's quick to buckle himself in, and for a moment I consider taking him. He won't have to know why I'm sneaking around. He can sit in the car. He can protect me from freaky women who like to hang themselves in my presence, and we can go out and eat donuts afterwards. It's made of win.

I shake myself back to reality.

"Get out of the car," I bark.

"OK, OK." He holds up his hands in an effort to quell my aggression.

"I mean thanks, but I can't drive anyone under twenty-one for the next two decades. It's a special stipulation on my driver's permit."

His forehead wrinkles.

"Liar, liar pants on fire," he says it calm and eerily out of cadence. "You're going to see Logan. He's not the right one for you, but have it your way." He gets out of the car.

I roll down the window.

"What do you mean?" I shout after him.

"I mean, I am." He holds out his arms while walking backward up the driveway.

Dream on.

Nicholas Haver lives behind the gates.

Shit.

I slam my hand against the steering wheel.

The guard at the gate all but laughed when I told him I was going to visit my friend Nick. He went over the list twice before making me circle back around to the main road. Then it hits me. Ellis Harrison.

I fly back down to the house, which eats up another twenty minutes and find Ellis standing in a circle of smoke with two guys I don't know.

"Ellis," I hiss.

The whites of his eyes glint.

"You got food?" He asks with glassy eyes.

The air smells funny. I see one of the guys pass a joint to the other, and I take in a sharp breath.

"You guys can't do this here!" I try to ventilate the area with my hands. "I'm going to go to jail or prison for this. Plus my mom is totally going to kill me!"

"Relax." Ellis snaps out of his stupor and looks surprisingly normal.

"I changed my mind. I want you to come with." I drag him by the elbow and shove him into the passenger seat.

I run around to the other side and click on my seatbelt.

"Buckle up," I yell, backing out the driveway in haste.

"Where we headed?"

"Your place."

"There's no food at my place."

"We're not headed there for the food." I try to sound mysterious like maybe he might get lucky, so he won't protest and screw up my chances of getting behind the gates. Nicholas Haver's house is miles away from the front gate, and I don't much like running around the dark in the middle of the night.

We drive in silence. Or at least I think we do until he lets out a loud series of strange noises and I realize he's snoring.

I shake him abruptly as we arrive at the gate.

"Help you?" The guard asks peering into the car.

"I'm taking Ellis Harrison home. Right, Ellis?"

He gazes at the night security guard through heavily lidded eyes.

"Hey there." The security guard gives a brief salute as the barricade rises.

I roll past the guardhouse and into the quiet solitude of the backcountry of Paragon Estates.

I'm in.

I'm going to the faction council meeting—with a very stoned Ellis Harrison.

24

Just Call Me Angel

"Over there on the right." Ellis points to his house, bright eyed and bushy tailed.

I pass it up trying to visualize the map, which I stupidly forgot to bring with me. I know he lives on a cul-de-sac called Saddle Drive, and he's the only house on the block so it can't be that hard to find. It veered right off Steamboat, which is the main thoroughfare.

"Turn around right here," he instructs.

"I'm not going to your house. Would you like me to drop you off?"

"No," he says suspiciously. "You passed up his house too." His being Logan's.

"Not going there either. I need to pick up something for a friend at Nicholas Haver's house. You know him?"

"Big Nick?" There's a note of disbelief in his tone.

"Yeah, big Nick. So what does big Nick do anyway?" No point in letting my imagination run wild if Ellis is willing to blab.

"Construction."

"Oh right. That makes total sense." Not really.

Ellis instructs me on the details of how to get there, and after several twists and turns down unmarked roadways I come to realize there is no way I could have gotten here on my own. So it's sort of a God thing Ellis is with me.

The street is loaded with cars. I park high up on the ridge behind a giant shrub and get out of the minivan.

Ellis joins me.

"You mind waiting in the car?"

"You're parked like a mile away. I'll come with. Besides, I like Nick. I helped him do an addition last spring."

"OK. But I have to tell you something. I'm not really here to get anything from Nick. I have to ask you to wait by the car. This is strictly female business. I'm actually here to see his wife." Who I pray actually exists.

His face darkens.

"Well if you put it that way." He leans against the minivan and crosses his arms.

Stay, I shout at him mentally as though he were a dog.

It's beyond dark, so I open up my cell and let it illuminate a pathway over to the property. I round out the back and find a giant structure, like Ellis's pool house only ten times that size. The lights are on, and I can see a bunch of heads sprinkled around the room.

I tiptoe across the long stretch of yard with no bushes, or trees, or structure to obscure me. I glide across something greasy with my left foot, and it's not until the foul odor hits my nose that I realize I stepped in a pile of dog droppings.

Gross.

I smear my shoe along the grass until I work most of it off.

If there's dog crap, where's the dog?

I don't waste any time analyzing the situation, instead I hug the back wall, slightly out of breath from the long trek over.

Voices emanate from inside.

The window clear on the opposite end is open so I get on all fours and crawl over.

I can hear them perfectly clear as if I were in the room.

"Noster can't afford to side with Celestra," a male voice says matter of fact—sounds bored, actually.

Gee thanks.

"So Celestra is on its own?" Sounds like Logan. "Then don't threaten me with a trial by Justice Alliance when I take things into my own hands."

He's yelling. I don't think I've ever seen Logan worked up, let alone, yell.

"What in the heck?" A voice hisses from behind.

I turn in fright to see Ellis Harrison nose to nose with me, and I let out a small squeal.

A dog comes charging out of the bushes, two glowing red eyes—teeth sharp as arrows, barking at top volume. He's charging a million miles an hour, all rage and salivating fangs.

I can't look, so I push my face into Ellis' chest.

A chain rattles severely, and the dog yelps a series of whimpers. When I look up he's only three feet away, impotent to complete his mission.

Bodies bleed out of the room, and a man with a belly that hangs clear over his trousers yanks Ellis up by one hand and me by the other.

"What in the..." he says full of surprise.

It's Gage I see first.

"She's here for me," Gage shouts, making his way over.

Logan comes into focus, his eyes the size of baseballs.

"All of you out," Nicholas Haver shouts, pushing Ellis and I in their direction.

Just a minute ago the patio was teeming with people and now there's just the four of us. It's like they scurried back inside because they didn't want to be seen.

"I'm not here for them," I say with a renewed vigor.

Big Nick eyeballs me up and down.

"I'm here because I belong here." I stop short of flaunting the word Celestra because of Ellis, who, by the way, ruined everything.

"Come on." Logan grabs me by the waist and starts leading me back up the trail.

What the hell are you doing here? He sounds markedly pissed.

I need more answers than you're willing to give me. I give his hand a hard squeeze to let him know I feel the exact same way.

And you bring Ellis? He glowers over at him openly.

I needed to get behind the gates. Besides, he's stoned. He won't remember half this tomorrow.

He'll clearly remember all this tomorrow, and by the way—he's always stoned. That's baseline for him. He twitches his nose. *New perfume?*

Yes. It's called Craptastic. Like my night.

We get back up to the ridge and I take in a few deep lungfuls of fresh night air. I pluck off my shoes and toss them in a plastic bag that I find floating around the trunk of the minivan.

"Are you guys coming back to the party?" I ask looking from Logan to Gage.

"No." Logan observes as Ellis stumbles into the passenger side of the minivan. "And neither are you."

He takes the keys I'm holding rather loosely and hands them over to Gage.

"Drive Ellis back. Stay as long as you want, but drive his car home for him." He turns to me. "You're coming with me."

25

Facts

The shutters are drawn and a small glow of light warms the Oliver's sprawling estate.

"Nobody's home," he informs as we enter through the front.

A lethargic yellow lab wags his tail nervously as he sniffs forcibly by my feet.

"You must be Charlie." He was out back in the fields when I was here the other day, so we missed our first meeting.

Logan leads me into the dining room. A palatial rectangle sits in the middle with a gold inlaid table that's fit to seat twelve comfortably. A massive hutch sits behind it, and on each of the glass shelves are hundreds of angel figurines. My mother would say the whole thing's gaudy, but I find it fascinating—eccentric.

"I'd have to agree with her." Logan rubs his thumb against my hand.

"Is there any way to turn that off?" I seem to keep forgetting he can hear me clear as a loud speaker.

"Not that I know of." He pulls out a sheet of paper and a pen from a small desk off to the side before we take a seat at the table.

He starts making charts and jotting down names. The word faction is written in giant letters across the top.

"So you're finally going to tell me everything there is to know?" I'm thrilled by the prospect.

"Maybe." He keeps at his work until he's done. "I'd never lie to you."

"So that means no."

"That means maybe." He looks almost apologetic.

He spins the paper around and scoots in close.

"There are five factions of earthbound angels." He taps his pen against the first one. "Celestra—that's us." A brief impression of a smile appears. "Countenance, most powerful, crooked bunch of bastards that roam the earth—think mob, but far more greedy. We don't know who they are. They don't make it a practice to reveal their status. They band together and share the wealth, so there're lots of reasons for keeping their mouths shut. Plus, they don't frown upon killing their own if they don't cooperate. Then there's the most common three, Noster, Levatio—that's Gage and my uncle. Deorsum, that's my aunt. And there you have it, factions at a glance."

"So Celestra has the most powerful blood?"

"Yes."

"Which means?" I can tell I'm going to have to pull all of the answers out of him, which isn't fair because I don't know the right questions to ask.

"Which means if there were enough of us, we could rule the Nephilim kingdom. Celestra is supposedly in charge but with lame duck status. It's like a government, and right now the crooks are taking over. Each faction must pay a royalty to the Counts in exchange for their protection."

"Protection against what? Aren't they the ones we need protection from?"

He points the pen in my face.

"You're a smart one. Technically, yes, but they claim to be protecting us against other spiritual beings called, Sectors. The Sectors are like overlords of the angel armies. You're a warrior if you hadn't already done your homework. That's why it's all right to kill if your life is in danger, or you've been instructed to do so by your faction leader."

"And is that a sufficient plea to tell your legal council before they haul your ass to prison?"

"You won't go to prison if you stay within those bounds. The factions take care of everything."

"So murder out of necessity or under orders is OK."

"Essentially."

"I don't exactly understand the Sectors," I say.

"I don't either. It falls under the category of wait until you're thirty, but I have some theories."

"And what about powers? Both you and Gage are really strong. Gage knows things. You and I can read minds, what else is there?"

"My aunt can influence small children to do her bidding. She owns and operates the single largest daycare center on the island. Parents love her. Most Deorsum don't have that ability. The run of the mill things for them are strength and speed. You might say they got the shaft when it comes to outstanding superpowers."

"I hear pretty well, too." A tall brunette with her hair in a bun makes her way over and extends her hand.

She's wearing a royal blue suit and has on an obnoxious shade of orange lipstick, but she's absolutely stunning. I'd love for my mom to meet her.

"Emma." Her fingers are frozen, so limp she barely moves within my seemingly harsh grasp.

"Skyla."

Logan's uncle enters and gives a slight wave. He looks over my shoulder and nods.

"Giving her the breakdown I see. I should have the blood work completed in a weeks time. I'm running a very detailed panel, that way we'll know for sure if you're Celestra or a mix or anything at all. Sometimes that happens. But if you're a mix we go by what you have more of. It's just easier for labeling purposes."

"Great. I look forward to it."

They exit with polite nods and smiles. Second thought, my mother would eat her for breakfast, and Tad would embarrass the hell out of me. It's probably best they never meet. But of course now that I don't want them to...

"We should have your parents over," Logan suggests as though he's just had some great epiphany.

"Is one of your abilities causing super humiliation?"

He frowns.

"They'll meet one day." He starts drawing boxes around all the faction names. "Levatio. The lucky bastards as I like to call them."

"Are they lucky?" I'm fascinated to learn more about them, especially since Gage is one.

"Not really. They've got strength and speed, the knowing, teleportation."

"How cool is that?" Now I totally wish Gage were here so he could bolt around the room.

"Noster's same as Levatio with the exception they can see through walls, and oh yeah, both can levitate."

"As in fly?"

"It's not long range or anything, they can't orbit the earth, but yes."

"That's so freaking fantastic," I say dazzled by all these strange superpowers.

He drops his pen and folds his hands together.

"And what about us?" I take hold of his eyes with mine. An electrical current sizzles between us. He's stunning and sharp, and annoyingly outright elusive with information.

"Read minds." He holds out his hands and shrugs. "Strength, speed." His expression clouds over. "Time travel."

26

Principles

Time travel.

The word goes off like a gong long after Logan expelled it. He said he couldn't really elaborate, that maybe we could talk about it later so I just let it go. Just the idea was enough to satiate me for now.

Gage comes in at three in the morning and says the exact words I don't want to hear.

"Party's still going strong."

"We should get back there." I spike up on the couch and stab my eyes around in the dark, in an effort to wake up. Logan put on a DVD, and then we started kissing and I must have fallen asleep.

I look over at Logan totally embarrassed and guilty.

"I really do love kissing you," I say stupidly.

He looks mildly amused.

"Stay here," Logan pulls me in, "you're going to want to kick everyone out. No point in being a buzz kill. Besides, it'll be four by the time we get there."

He's right.

"I won't be able to sleep knowing they're destroying the house."

"Nobody's destroying anything." Gage flops on the couch opposite us. "Ellis was having a goodtime, didn't want to come home."

"You have a goodtime?" I'd feel kind of bad if Gage said no. There were tons of girls there—girls that would have been supermodels back home, raking in millions.

A twinge of jealousy cinches in my stomach, and I shake my head trying to get rid of the feeling. I'm into Logan. I don't need Gage. I couldn't care less if he were with ten girls at once.

"So you up on all the celestial B.S.?" He asks.

"It's not B.S.," I shoot back. My father was one, and I don't like him talking that way.

"Sorry." He covers the top of his head with a pillow. "You guys try anything out?"

I shake my head. Logan, for whatever reason, doesn't seem that into exploring powers with me.

"Maybe I'll help you out sometime," Gage offers.

"Maybe you won't," Logan counters.

"I want to," I say. "I want to try things out. And you said my powers could grow. It's like a muscle, right? The more you use it the stronger it gets?"

"No." The whites of Logan's eyes widen. "The more you use it the more trouble you can get into. Definitely not like that."

"I know enough to be careful."

"You know enough to be dangerous," Logan speeds it out.

We sit there with our eyes glinting back and forth at one another like ping-pongs.

I don't like the chains of restraint Logan puts over me. I'm not an infant, and according to Gage, I can't get myself killed.

I look from Logan to Gage. I might have to take Gage up on his offer. It's Logan's own fault if I end up going behind his back.

I want to know what I'm capable of. I want to feel it. And if I really can time travel, maybe I can save my father?

Sunday afternoon I head back home.

Gage was right. The house wasn't destroyed. It was merely decimated.

I walk stunned from room to room. The kitchen has a lawn chair I've never seen before dangling out of the sink.

The couch is configured differently in the living room and every single cushion is nowhere to be seen. The curtains have been yanked down on one side, and there's a clear slit down the center where the light comes through, and if its mocking me.

"I'm toast." I sludge through empty beer bottles and soda cans, mystery wrappers and some unidentifiable things until I hit the stairs. A trail of dark liquid has been poured on the first five steps, and something gummy is stuck to the rest of the carpet leading on up.

I check Drake's room first. His bed is unmade and to tell the truth I have no clue if that's normal. Mia and Melissa's room looks untouched. Both bunks are still laden with stuffed animals arranged face out and in size order, so that's a no. Next is my room.

My freaking room.

Brielle is sprawled out on the bed stark naked with her shoes still on. I run over and throw my t-shirt on her from off the floor in an effort to cover the insanity.

"You sleep with somebody in here?" I don't really care that she cheated on Drake, it's just that I'm going to have to burn the bed, that's all.

She gives a guilty laugh, bearing her teeth in an awkward manner a little too long.

I head back into the hall and shut the door tight. Thank God Logan didn't venture in behind me.

My parent's room is next. The door sticks, and my heart drops thinking someone might be bolted in there. I bust through and there's no one except one very rumpled bed and I'm absolutely positive my anal, male chauvinist pig of a stepfather would not have allowed my mother to leave it this way. He'd hogtie her in apron strings and chain her to the bedpost if she tried to get away with crap like this.

"I'm going to die. My parents are going to execute the world's harshest judgment upon me and I'll never leave the house again. We need to go back in time," I plead to Logan.

He shakes his head looking mournful over the situation.

"You can't use that for something like this. It falls under domestic detail. I'll call Gage. We'll clean up as much as we can."

Nat and Kate swing by as well. We manage to get all the trash off the floors and recover all but one of the sofa cushions. It looks toothless, with three brown cushions and one white gaping space with nothing but the spring cover below.

I collect the bedding from Mom and Tad's room and start the wash. It's going to take three hours before I wash all of those fat, fuzzy blankets, and that oversized comforter will never dry by tonight.

"I might be homeless after today." I let Logan cradle me in the living room. I find his lips and forget about the whole mess my life has turned into.

The front door jiggles, and a pair of footsteps make their way over.

I look up expecting to see Gage or Bree or anyone else. But I don't. Instead I see my mother.

Red Handed

Tad, Drake, and the girls tumble in after my mom.

"*Skyla Laurel Messenger*, get yourself upstairs now," she shrieks. "And excuse me, mister who kisses my daughter in my living room, you can find the front door thank you very the hell much!" Her voice hits that upper register I haven't heard in years since she had one of her famous blowouts with my father.

I head on up and pause at the top.

"Oh, my, word," she screams.

I can hear her roaming deeper and deeper, and now Tad is shouting something, and they seem to be shouting in unison and at each other at the same time. I see Nat and Kate leave. Logan's truck rolls down the driveway, so Gage must have went out the back.

"What's going on?" Brielle staggers out of my bedroom.

I motion her back inside and press my finger to my lips.

Mia and Melissa gallop upstairs lugging their overnight bags.

"You're in deep shit," Mia whispers as they saunter past me.

Drake comes up and sees Brielle.

"Cool." He relaxes into a dorky grin and they go off in his room together.

I can't believe this. I let Brielle convince me into doing something that I knew, I *knew*, was a very bad idea. I feel like beating myself, giving myself black eyes over the entire event, but I know my mother will probably do that for me.

Heavy footsteps ignite in this direction. I duck into my bedroom and shut myself in.

A choir of disappointed murmurs buzz through the other side of the door, then a violent shriek when my mother, most likely, sees her unmade bed.

My door swings open and I huddle in the corner fearing for my life.

"Get out here now." She annunciates every single word.

Reluctantly I exit the safety of my bedroom and head into the hall.

"Who did you have in this house this weekend? And I know that lot of not so innocent looking kids helping you clean was just the tip of the iceberg."

"All the trashcans are filled with beer bottles," Tad shouts.

"Skyla!" My mother rages.

"I didn't drink. I swear!"

"Well bully for you," Mom sings. "That means I had a bunch of drunk teenagers at my house, and if anything happens to them because of their little trip to Landon tavern, it's on my head!"

I shrink back. I hate seeing my mother this mad. I hate the sound of her voice when it's locked in anger.

"Did you have sex with that boy here?"

"No." My hands fly up over my ears. We've definitely drifted into the relationship no-fly zone. "I'm a virgin. I swear." File that under things I never thought I'd scream out loud.

"Yeah, well, too bad there's no surefire way to tell because I really don't believe you."

And there's another riff in our already deteriorating relationship.

"She's probably on drugs, too." Tad paces in a frantic circle. I bet he regrets marrying my mother, regrets the sloppy baggage she dragged into it like some stench-riddled carcass.

"And why is the minivan parked in the street?" My mother demands.

"Because the driveway was full." There, I said the truth.

"You don't have a license." I can feel the heat of her breath as she roars an inch from my nose.

"And it smells like a bear took a shit in there." Tad matches her tone.

"Maybe it did," I offer.

"There are no bears on Paragon," Tad screams into me on his way to the bedroom.

I can hear the shower turn on from Drake's room. He's probably in there with the hellion responsible for this carnage while I occupy the 'rents with my Brielle-inspired shenanigans. I'm suddenly regretting we ever met.

"Get to your room until I think of an ample and just punishment." Disappointment seethes from her pores, all directed right at me.

"You ever wish I was in that car with Dad?" The words tumble from my lips bypassing the brain filter on their way out.

"Skyla," her whole affect softens, "don't ever say that." She pulls a loose strand of hair and tucks it behind my ear. "I knew you were probably going to have a party."

Great. She thinks the worst of me. Technically it was Brielle who had the party, Brielle who had sex in my bed, and Brielle who's most likely doing that exact same thing right now under her nose.

"When I was your age I did the same thing."

"Oh." I can't even imagine my mother my age. "You get in trouble?"

"No. I never got caught."

I raise my fingers over my mouth in surprise.

"I clean better than you." She walks down the hall to her bedroom and shuts the door.

I head over to Drake's room and knock on the door to give them a scare. A scrambling sound emits from inside, then silence.

No reason Brielle should have all the fun, although being with Drake is technically a punishment. Obviously she's a sadist.

I head over to my room and close the door.

My mother—I track through my memory trying to recall her ever mentioning her youth. I know she grew up near the waterfront. My grandparents died a few years back. She has a sister in Idaho. That's all I really know about my mom. Is she a member of an angel faction? How exactly does one go about asking their mother if they are, in any way, a supernatural being?

I yank the covers off my bed and drop onto the bare mattress.

I don't know how, but I'm going to make it a point to find out.

28

Ninjas

Days drag on. I familiarize myself with the nuances of my bedroom. Sometimes I sit in the walk-in closet with the lights off and text Logan for hours. Apparently ample punishment doesn't include taking away my cell or my computer. I'm thrilled actually. My room feels more like a safe haven rather than a prison.

My mother gives a mild knock before entering.

"You up for a chore?"

"Yes," I say hesitantly. Obviously no would have been the wrong answer. I try to assess her mood, but the only clue as to how she might be feeling is that bright pink ruffled shirt. It screams take-me-to-the-circus-and-put-me-on-the-first-clown-you-see.

"I need to do a bunch of paperwork for Tad, so I'm going to ask you to take Mia and Melissa back-to-school shopping for me.

I perk up at the thought. Outside? In a car?

"I'll drop you guys off, just call when you need to get picked up. I know it seems like I'm going soft on you, but summer's going to end in a couple weeks." She lets her shoulders rise and fall. "Who knows, maybe I am getting soft. Be ready in fifteen."

I flip off my bed and text Logan. I think we're about to have an accidental meeting.

I pretend to absorb myself in a novel on the way to the mall, so my mother might hold off on the inquisition. I'm still waiting for a thorough line of questioning involving Logan since she caught us in a heavy-duty lip lock.

We file out of the van, and I wave her off. Mia and Melissa are armed with cash, and per my mother's wicked plan, I am not. I didn't fight my mother on that one. I'm sure new clothes are in the cards for me, just not today, or perhaps not 'till I'm thirty.

We head into the Paragon West End mall. It's busier than the last time I was here by several hundred people. Must be the end of summer sale and back to school bustle all rolled into one. I see Logan over by the giant fountain and wave.

"OK. So you guys are going to stick together, and you have enough money for lunch and a movie, right?"

"Oh, we can totally see a movie!" Melissa clutches my sister's arm.

"Or two or three," I suggest. "Look, I have my cell. Just call me when you're ready to go. I'm going to hang out, kay?"

They wander down the corridor and disappear into a juniors dress shop, bubbling with excitement.

I envy Mia. I wish I had a sister my age rather than Drake. At least I have Logan to take the edge off.

He greets me with a kiss.

"Let's blow this joint." I tick my head toward the parking lot. The last thing I need is spotting Mia and Melissa every five minutes. They're totally safe. I can feel it in my creaky bones. It's not like I left them alone—they're not seven. They're thirteen.

"So where you taking me?" We've got the windows rolled down and the wind thrashes my hair around.

"It's a surprise."

We drive for a half hour past the falls. I'm completely nervous about how far away I've gotten from the girls. He pulls down a tiny dirt road with a big white-planked sign that reads Black Forest.

It's more than a thicket of pine trees. It's a denseness that I've never seen before. Walls of emerald fur line the roadway impenetrable by man or beast.

He drives down to a clearing, and we get out of the truck.

"You take all the girls here?" Really I don't want an answer to that one.

"I don't think I've taken anyone here." He leads me down a small stone path that leads into a smaller clearing, deep in the forest where you could feasibly only arrive on foot.

"It's kind of creepy." Even though I'm with Logan, I feel entirely vulnerable.

Don't. We're safe. He walks over and snaps a one foot round branch off a tree, easy as snapping a pretzel.

Words garble in my throat. I can't seem to push any of them out.

"I'm going to teach you how to do that." He launches into one of his wild grins.

"I'm all ears." I walk over and stand next to him.

"First, you determine that you can do this. Before you choose what you're going to do with your strength, you need to believe."

"OK. So I believe I can pluck this branch off." I choose a far smaller, more meager branch to target.

He motions for me to try.

I give it a yank, and it snaps upwards with violent force. Nada.

"You have to really believe. It's a biblical principle. You need to come from a place of knowing. Really understand that you've been given the power, and if you doubt it's possible—it will be impossible."

"Great." I try branch after branch, each time targeting something softer, meeker. "Can't do it." I suck in deep full breaths. It's too exhausting to even think about trying again.

"OK." He looks around at the bed of dead pine needles on the ground. "Let's try speed." He positions himself like he's going to run, but ends up standing next to a tree hundreds of yards away.

"Hey! How'd you do that?" I yell, exhilarated.

He cups his hands around his mouth. "Try it!"

I place myself in the identical position, and start in on a run. The whole world turns into a blur, a carefree whirl on a familiar carnival ride. It reminds me of when my father used to take me up in his arms and spin me. Or at least I thought he was spinning me—it felt just like this.

I appear right next to Logan with my chest heaving from the mammoth effort.

"You did it!" He wraps his arms around my waist and gives me a twirl.

A loud reverberating shot rings out in the forest. A branch the size of a small tree just above our heads begins its silent tumble right for us.

Logan pushes me out of the way as the timber crashes onto the bed of pine needles.

"That could have killed us!" I pant. My heart rattles in my chest like a caged rabid squirrel.

He looks around calm with careful intent.

"I believe that was the plan."

29

Trouble

Logan and I perch behind the trunk of an evergreen while staring out into the heavy shadow of the surrounding forest.

Logan leans forward and brings his finger to his lips while looking at one of the branches on a tree across the way. He throws his finger into the air with a hard point. A dark-winged creature bolts out and heads to the west.

"It's that raven," I marvel. "What is that, your bird or something?"

"It sends a signal."

"Can't you just use your cell?"

"It's more than that." He gets up on his feet. "C'mon." He pulls me in behind him using his body as a shield, and we walk light footed through the dense overgrowth. It's getting progressively darker. The fog illuminates itself like a lantern as it fills in the landscape around us.

The heavy crush of leaves quickens in our direction. A stench of rotting flesh, or putrid fish, clogs up my nostrils, and I find myself fighting the strong urge to vomit.

"What is that?"

"It's a Fem." He clutches at my shoulders. "We have to outrun it, or it'll kill us."

"I can't." I'm gonna die. My mother is going to find me in forest eaten by a Fem. "It's going to eat me, isn't it?" A weak groan emits from my throat.

"It might." He looks around distressed, panting.

He picks me up and starts running. It feels like trees are darting in and out of our path. The sky appears and disappears like lightning. I close my eyes and bury my face in Logan's chest until it feels like I'm flying in a dizzy circle with my father again. That's how Logan makes me feel—safe like my father.

An unbearably loud roar explodes right over my head, like that of a lion or a bear. I open my eyes to discover it emanating from Logan. I don't know whether to be frightened or entertained.

He jumps branch to branch, with me dangling on for dear life, and sits me a good twenty feet up. If I fall, I could easily crack my skull on the waiting rocks below.

He lunges forward and clutches at a dark figure.

I have no idea what in the hell it is. I've only seen the things of this world, and I know for certain this isn't one of them. I can't make out the proper form. When I see it, I sway in disbelief. I crouch in and hug the trunk with all my might.

A large bear looking creature ten feet high at least, with the girth of five bears up top, and legs like a jackrabbit, lunges and hisses at Logan. It looks like something out of a horror movie, something of pure evil. A shiny-flocked fur covers its flesh, its mouth is open, and it thrashes its bright red pit all over.

I close my eyes and bury my head into the trunk of the tree.

I can hear a scuffle take place, bodies being lifted and thrown to the ground with violent force. The unnatural quiver of the forest lets me know this is no ordinary match. This isn't human against human. And I have a very distinct feeling, that for one of them, this is going to end very, very, badly.

"Skyla!" Logan calls my name.

It takes all my effort to open my eyes and look in his direction. It might be his dying breath—the last word that leaves his mouth might be my name.

Logan's standing right there in the clearing with one foot on top of the beast's chest in triumph.

"You kill it?" I ask hesitantly.

"Take a picture."

"You're insane if you think I'm digging around for my phone."

Gage appears beneath me. "Jump, and I'll catch you."

"No." I strengthen my death grip on the trunk of the tree. "I'm very afraid of heights. I'll need hours of therapy to repair the damage done here today."

Logan springs up next to me and grabs me by the waist. That weightless feeling I hate flips through my stomach, and somehow we magically appear on terra firma.

The beast hisses, and a wall of vapors surround it before it evaporates into thin air. The horrible smell penetrates the forest, and we're forced to cover our mouths as we run for the car.

"Smells like raw sewage," I say as Logan helps me into the cab of his truck and shuts the door.

Gage appears in the seat next to me.

He pulls a small sprig of pine needles out of my hair and holds it out as if he were offering me a gift. He sneaks a quick kiss on my forehead.

"I'm glad you're OK," he whispers before disappearing.

Logan climbs in and shuts the door still out of breath.

"What exactly is a Fem, and please tell me that was the last one."

"A Fem can change shapes to be whatever it wants—whatever it thinks will frighten you and weaken your defenses."

Immediately I think of the woman with crazy hair, hanging outside my kitchen door.

"And what do they want?"

"They personally don't want anything. They're a lower faction of the Sectors. They do all the spiritual dirty work. It's been long believed that Countenance hire them out to do their bidding, but of course they deny it. There's not enough evidence to bring them to the Justice Alliance."

"You said they hire them out. What's their currency?"

"It's a power exchange. I don't know how it works. All I know is if you ever come upon a Fem—one of you will be leaving dead."

"I could never kill anything like that. I'd be too afraid."

"That's why it looks the way it does because it wants to scare you. You have to remember it's nothing more than a ball of air."

"Ball of air." I repeat the words. But it looked so real—fought so hard.

I don't think I have what it takes to be an angel. Somehow, I don't think it matters.

30

Snatched

It's dark by the time we get to the mall. We made a pit stop at Logan's house so he could shower and change. All the hundreds of shoppers who were here this afternoon have gone, and it looks like a bona fide ghost town.

I call Mia on her cell but it goes to voicemail, same with Melissa.

Not two minutes later, my mother calls and informs me she's picking us up—that it's nearing our bedtime. I leave the word bedtime out of my lexicon when I translate the conversation to Logan.

"So you're like a superhero," I push into him playfully.

"So are you." He gives a playful shove back before circling my waist.

"Yeah, but you killed a dragon. That practically makes you a prince."

"It wasn't a dragon, but it might be next time." He looks resigned to this. "And if I'm a prince, you must be a princess."

I reach up and give a supple kiss to his neck.

"It's pretty amazing that we're both Celestra. We could have an entire faction of perfect Celestrial beings running around one day."

"Or flying. We could always learn to fly."

"So we can learn other gifts?"

"Yeah, but it's like learning the piano for the very first time or another language. It takes great effort to master it. With your natural gifts, you just need to believe. He does the rest for you."

"Who's he?"

"Master." He points up.

Before we can continue on with our conversation, my cell goes off. It's Mom.

"I'm right here in the parking lot. Come on down." There's a hint of impatience in her voice.

I hang up, struck with panic.

"I have to find the girls."

Logan and I buy movie tickets just so we can get in. We comb through a football field of blackened movie theaters. I'm so desperate I'm shouting their names as I walk in without regard for the movie or the patrons. To make matters worse, it's nearing ten o'clock, and I keep ignoring my mother's nagging phone calls.

I meet Logan back outside by the concession stand.

"They're not anywhere." A quiver of fear bubbles through me. I can feel the tears building fast. "You think someone took them?"

A hard knock explodes on the glass wall facing outside. It's my mother with an irate expression, violently waving me over.

I walk past Logan mouthing a goodbye and head out in the cold damp air to meet her.

"It's that boy again, isn't it?" Her eyes expand the size of dishes. "Instead of a nice day out with your sisters, you turned this into some sort of romantic rendezvous!"

I hardly consider slaying a beast in the woods a romantic rendezvous.

"No," I object just above a whisper.

"Where are your sisters?"

Again she's exasperated. I bet I'll hear later how she did the exact same things when she was younger, but judging by the intense venomous glare—maybe not.

Just as I'm about to admit I've badly misplace both Mia and Melissa, my cell goes off.

"Mia!" I hold it up triumphantly.

"So what movie did you see?" I try to act nonchalant as though I knew they were in the theater all along, which I sort of did.

"Emma Fantastic," she chortles into my ear.

"Emma Fantastic," I say, covering the phone. Both my mother and I turn to the display board to see what time Emma Fantastic gets out, only to find out after checking everything twice, Emma fucking Fantastic isn't playing at the theater.

"Listen, I don't know what you're trying to pull, but I have Mom here and we're both well aware Emma Fantastic isn't playing." I try asserting my authority in an effort to impress my mother.

"I know it's not playing there." Mia always sounds about seven on the phone, so it's impossible to stay mad at her. "We took a bus to the East mall on the other side of the island."

My fingers shake as I glance over at my mother nervously. Something tells me it's going to be a long car ride over.

And you know what? I was right.

It takes over forty-five minutes with no traffic before we turn into the parking lot. My mother has gone over every single horrifying scenario of what might have happened to the girls. Who knew the harrowing possibilities were seemingly endless? Of course she left out being eaten by a giant, smelly Fem, but she couldn't have guessed that in a million years.

It occurs to me that I missed a thousand opportunities on the way over to politely nudge her and ask if she was an angel. At this point Mia and Melissa are in as much trouble as I am, so things couldn't possibly get any worse.

"Mom? Remember when Dad would call me his angel? Why do you think that was?"

"Because you hadn't bloomed into your teenage years." She honks the horn as she pulls against the curb.

Mia and Melissa startle in our direction with the flash of the headlights.

"Besides," she continues, "he loved making you into something special. Mia too, but your relationship with your dad was different. It's like you shared some special bond. He said you would surpass him in greatness someday." She shakes a pang of grief away.

Mia and Melissa pile in the backseat. My mother turns up the volume on her glacial queen routine, and we start in on a rather quiet ride home.

I lean my head against the cool glass of the window and watch the stars turn and dance with every new twist in the road. I wonder if my father's watching me, watching me kiss Logan, and shiver in fear while perched in the branches of trees. I wonder what he thinks of all this. I wonder if he really cares anymore.

31

Leave

I text Logan as soon as I get back up in my room, and let him know I survived— for now.

He texts me back. **I'm staying in tonight.**

As opposed to? ~S

Lexy Bakova's party. Gage wanted me to go with, but I said no.

Aww. He doesn't want to piss me off, so he stayed in. So wise.

Thanx ~S

So what are you wearing?

Flannel pants with a hole in the thigh, and a ragged old sweat shirt that I've used to do yard work in.

You're a pervert, you know that? ~S

I was hoping you'd notice. I can practically hear him saying it.

There's a soft knock on the door.

Brb. I drop my cell on the bed and scramble to a seated position.

It's Drake.

"What?" I say annoyed, picking my phone back up and cradling it.

"I'm going out tonight, and I want you to come."

"You're going out where?" I ask suspiciously.

"Some party at some cheerleader's house. Brielle wants me to go, and I don't really know anyone like you do."

"You just said Brielle's going."

"What if she leaves me?" He runs his hands through his hair in a panic.

"She most likely will," I say it matter of fact. "Besides, I can't. I'm grounded, like forever."

"So what more could they do to you? And it's not like you're going to get caught. How many times do they come in your room at night to check on you?"

Never. I start rotating the idea around in my brain.

"We can come back early. And they're already asleep," he adds.

Mom did mention how exhausted she was when we pulled into the driveway. Drake's right, she's probably being haunted in her dreams by Chloe as we speak.

"Give me ten minutes."

Drake thinks we should walk out the front door as opposed to climbing out the window and swinging down to earth on tree branches like I suggested. Turns out we manage to arouse the suspicions of no one as we make our way to the minivan where Brielle is already waiting.

"I can't believe you're sneaking out!" She hugs me as though I've accomplished something major.

"Drake has permission." I nod in an effort to aggravate him by removing some of the mystique he's trying to build.

"She knows," he gives a dirty look before unlocking the door.

Clearly the scent of crap does not dissipate as easily as one would think. We drive all the way there with the windows down. And it's not until I see Gage standing out front that I text Logan and tell him where I am.

Lexy lives just south of the mall, overlooking the ocean in a relatively normal sized home. It looks like the same crowd that was over at my house Saturday is circulating in the driveway. I recognize more than a few faces. I get out and make my way over to Gage.

He takes a full step back as though he's looking at an illusion.

"It's really me."

"You look," he pauses to take me in, "amazing."

"Thanks." I can feel the heat rising to my cheeks. "I just told Logan to come on down." It's starting to feel a little awkward, so I do a quick survey of the sea of people to try and spot Brielle. Not that I really want to hang with Drake. Maybe we can both ditch him.

"So you all right?" Gage has a soulful way about him. His hair is slicked back wet. The sliver of moonlight that's out tonight casts a perfect reflection off the top.

"I'm," I want to say fine, but what's the point? "Completely freaked out. I don't know what I'd have done if I was alone. For sure I wouldn't be standing here. I owe Logan my life," I gush.

His expression dims.

"I wouldn't go that far." He motions for me to follow.

We head toward the side of the house, barren of people. Gage leans in and places his hand on the wall behind me, pinning me in.

Something in my gut loosens, and I feel completely relaxed.

"So why don't you go in there and fight some of those girls off for a while?" Truth is, I'm afraid he's going to kiss me. Truth is, I'm afraid I'm not going to stop him.

"I don't want to be in there. I want to be out here. With you."

I look past his shoulder into the street. No sign of a car, not one single headlight going in either direction. A warm breeze wafts by, and the strong scent of eucalyptus fills the air.

"You know, I kind of have this thing going with Logan, and..." I let my gaze fall as his body moves closer to mine. I can feel the warmth radiating from his skin, hot as a fever.

"If I'm going to marry you one day," he says rather dreamily, "we're going to have to do this. A lot."

It's an explosion of emotion when his lips connect with mine. A love song, and every glorious sunset I've ever seen all rolled into one. We write a poem with the dull ache of our passion.

I snap back to reality and push back hard. He flies back a good three feet, surprised at how he got there.

I make a beeline for the front of the house where I find Logan talking to Michelle and Lexy.

"Hi," I try not to sound winded—like Gage's kiss didn't leave me breathless.

He takes a hold of the back of my neck.

White noise! White noise!

I try to focus on my breathing, the stars—his eyes.

I need to be with Michelle tonight. I'm getting very close.
My heart sinks like granite.

"I guess I'll see you around," I say maneuvering myself into the throngs of bodies.

32

Jealous

I can't stand watching him with Michelle. Why does he care so much about a stupid diary when it hurts me?

Gage follows me around like a puppy—an apologetic puppy who thrives on my attention.

"You know he's just using her, right?" I motion over to the two of them sitting by the roaring fire. Michelle has her arms around Logan's midsection, and he's caressing her neck. "He's just listening in," I say.

Gage doesn't appear too amused.

"I would never do that to you." There's something sincere in his tone, and I wholeheartedly believe him.

"Why does he want this diary so bad anyway?" I whisper.

"He thinks it has some vital piece of information."

"To what? Get her killers?"

He shakes his head.

"You know what they say about a fool?" He whispers.

"What?" I don't like how he's comparing Logan to a fool. He looks noble, like a king sitting over there. He has a glow about him that outshines the fire.

"Give him enough rope—he'll hang himself." Gage seems rather proud of his euphemism.

We watch as Michelle pulls his face down and kisses him full on the lips. He doesn't thrash around or toss her in the fire, instead he pulls back with nothing more than a blink—it makes me want to go over and knock both of them into the fire myself.

"He's gone too far." Hot angry tears burn the insides of my lids. I look around for signs of Drake or Brielle, but don't see any. They're probably rolling around in Lexy's bedroom. Brielle's not too shy when it comes to things like that. "Take me home."

"Sure."

The air outside has condensed a thin layer over everything. It leaves a fine mist over my skin and hair as we make our way over to Gage's truck. A black one to Logan's white, and easier to get into.

I'm so pissed I'm seething. I can't see straight, partially due to the tears I refuse to let fall. I push them away with the back of my hands.

"I don't really feel like going home." I haven't even been gone a full hour. If I get into trouble now I don't think any of this has been worth it. Tears shoot out the corner of my eyes, rapid fire. I can't seem to get a hold of myself. I start in on a full-blown sob into the palms of my hands, shaking like a freaking baby.

Gage pulls over and kills the ignition. He snaps off his seatbelt, then mine.

"Come here." He pulls me toward him and hands me a tissue from out of small box sitting on his console. "Look!" He marvels tracing the tail of a shooting star with his finger.

I wish I felt for Gage what I feel for Logan. I thought Logan and I had some stronger than steel impenetrable bond. I was already insanely attracted to him before I knew we were both Celestra.

I snuggle into Gage a little deeper.

One great thing about Gage is that he doesn't have the ability to know what I'm thinking. I don't have to infiltrate my brain with whitewash to get through a tough moment with him. It's a huge relief on many fronts.

He picks up my hand and inspects it.

"Are you sizing my finger?" I tease.

"No that's your other hand. I'm looking for trail marks."

"I don't think I got any scratches today."

His chest rises with restrained laughter. He holds my hand up to the moonlight streaming through the window. It looks pale, far too thin and fragile to be mine.

"Trail marks have to do with time travel. They're white dots that bleach into your skin. No one knows why they appear, they just do."

"Sort of like a passport." I muse joining him in examining my hands. "Is that one?"

Gage turns on the overhead light. "Son of a gun. It is." He hardly breaks out the enthusiasm when he says it. "Where'd you go?"

"I don't have a clue. I don't remember anything."

"You must have went somewhere. Think." He gives a gentle shake.

"Look there's another one." I say perfectly surprised by this revelation.

"You really get around don't you?" His dimples ignite on either side.

I reach up and turn off the overhead light. I don't want to think about how gorgeous Gage is, when the one I really want to be with is doing who knows what with Michelle, so he can get his hands on paper—*paper*.

"How'd you like the kiss?" He asks.

"It was all right." I give him a playful shove. Before I can say, don't do that again, his lips are covering mine. I don't back away or split his tongue in half with my teeth. I just let it happen. I don't feel half as guilty as before. A part of me wants to indulge. This might be the very last time I kiss him, ever.

It goes on for long stretches of time. We don't tire—just keep roaming around exploring, running our tongues back and forth, making lazy circles, figure eights.

Deep in my heart it doesn't feel right, like I'm cheating on Logan with no diary to gain from the whole experience. But I know it really doesn't matter. Relationships are fickle. I'm just fooling myself into thinking someone like Logan was going to stay with me exclusively. So what if he called himself my boyfriend? So what if I thought he really was? What do I know about love anyway?

A thunderous knock on the glass startles the two of us to attention.

Logan.

Gage opens the door. I'm not sure whether he gets out or Logan yanks him into the street, but a fight erupts. Full throttle kicks to the balls—punching. I see blood, and I don't know where it's coming from.

A pair of headlights stream over the two of them before slowing down. It's the minivan. I grab my purse and get out. I walk by their brawling bodies without once urging them to stop. I want Gage to beat the shit out of Logan. I hope that kiss hurt him as much as it did when I saw him with Michelle.

I get into the minivan and slam the slider door shut.

"Go around them," I tell Drake.

And he does.

33

Insurrection

I can feel my cell vibrate in my jeans as soon as I get back into my bedroom. It's Logan. If he thinks I'm going to engage in some lovelorn conversation until the wee hours of the morning—I glance up at the clock. It is the wee hours of the morning. I pick it up on the third ring.

"Make it quick."

"I'm sorry. Will you accept my apology?" He sounds hurt and sincere and incredibly sexy, but none of that rectifies the fact I can't get the visual of his lip-lock with Michelle out of my mind.

"No." I flick my heels off with a thump. "I'm just being honest."

"I wouldn't ask anything else."

I listen to the sound of his breathing until I feel hypnotized by the rhythm. I turn off the lamp next to my bed and lie under the covers with Logan tucked next to my ear in the dark.

"I wish I was with you. There's so much more I want to say," he whispers.

I hold the phone away while I sniff back tears.

"I made you cry." The anger in his voice resonates across the line. "You don't have to forgive me. I don't think I can forgive myself."

It crushes me to hear him say that. I heave a ragged breath into the pillow.

"Did you get the diary?"

"No."

"Are you done with trying?"

Nothing but silence.

"I guess I have my answer. Listen, I gotta go. Tell Gage I said hi, would you?"

I hope it hurt.

My mother has decided as a just punishment for losing track of my sisters I'm to play the part of the family scullery maid, forever.

I wash the stone floors in the kitchen and dining room with a mop and boiling hot water—literally boiling. She has me don a pair of black Wellies she dug out of the garage and has me heat the teakettle. Once it begins to scream from the pain, she instructs me to drizzle the scalding liquid all over the floor and scrub the crap out of it with a mop that's missing more than a few dozen threads. I'm beginning to think my mom is missing more than a few dozen brain cells because I don't see a darn of a difference on the blotchy brown floor.

"Mom?" I make sure the girls are outside before I continue the conversation.

"Mmm, hmm?" She doesn't look up from her crossword puzzle.

"Did you know that something terrible happened to a girl that used to live here?"

Her head shoots up. She folds over her crossword and leans in.

"Yeah, Hon, I do. It's part of the reason we were able to afford this house to begin with."

I stare over at her speechless. If it weren't for Chloe ending up at the bottom of Devil's Peak I wouldn't be standing here today. Fire sale.

"I also heard it was haunted." She sounds a little too exuberant over the subject.

I'd hate to burst her bubble by letting her know it was probably just a bunch of Fems running around trying to kill people.

"I wouldn't go sharing any of that with your sisters." Her lips make a perfect O as they run in through the backdoor.

"I'm trying to boil the floors here," I shout after them.

"You were always the funny one." Mom scrunches her nose over at me.

"I thought you were the funny one," I say. She married Tad, didn't she?

"Tell me about this boy you keep sneaking off to be with."

I freeze mid swipe. Does she mean sneaking off as in last night?

"His name is Logan." I swab the floors with long, clean strokes. "His parents died when he was young, and he lives with his aunt and uncle, one cousin the same age." I leave out the part about me kissing the both of them, and how I think I might have accidentally fallen in love so quickly—absentmindedly.

171

"You really like him don't you." It comes out a fact.

I shrug. The last thing I want to do is cry on my mother's shoulder over what happened last night.

"You're so young, Skyla. And beautiful!" She rises in her seat when she says it as though it were an epiphany. "There are so many fish in the sea. Don't settle for the first one that catches your eye. Play hard to get. You should be."

I don't really know what playing hard to get does for you, other than make you hard to get. Maybe if I were hard to get, Logan would be drooling all over me instead of Michelle.

The diary. That's exactly what Michelle's doing, playing hard to get. Unfortunately for me, it seems to be working.

"That girl that died, she and Logan used to go out," I add.

My mother drops her pen. "That's..." she searches the air for words. "Creepy." Her fingers strum across the granite. "That reminds me. Your father dated a girl who died unexpectedly."

My eyes bug out as I continue to swipe the floor—so much death and carnage. What's the purpose?

"Oh yeah? You know her name?" I ask.

"Candy something. Oh, it was probably something like Candace. They were seniors together."

I bet I could look her up in Dad's old yearbook. I bet if I dug around real good, I'd discover she was a Celestra.

34

Covetous

It's registration day at West Paragon, so Drake drives us down to campus to get our classes settled. Brielle is like a racehorse dying to get out of the gate to show us around.

I'm used to the practice field so I'm familiar with that much, but this time Brielle has us park in the main lot and we enter campus from an entirely different direction.

Stone cobbled pavers fan out in circular patterns that extend the entire length and breadth of the walkways. Two tall, brick buildings soften in a cloud of fog so thick you can hardly see the landscape beyond them. If I hadn't been here for cheer practice, I would never have known the buildings are encased in trees that stretch hundreds of feet into the air like javelins.

Brielle leads us into the shorter of the two buildings. Inside it's filled with all of the familiar faces from the parties I've been going to. I see Gage and Logan finishing up toward the front of the line. I try to pretend not to notice when I see them making their way over.

Ellis Harrison steps into my line of vision. He's sporting wireless glasses and a plaid shirt. I hardly recognize him with the clear eyes and the stony expression.

"I got you in two classes," he boasts.

"How do you know?" I try to ignore both Logan and Gage standing off to the side.

"It's posted up on the wall."

"Oh. I thought we were registering."

"Nope, just copying a list they were too lazy to email. Plus this way they get you to sign up for the after school stuff without infringing on their precious time."

Gage and Logan continue to wait patiently.

"So, what classes do we have together?" I widen my smile. Maybe if they think I'm suddenly interested in Ellis they'll leave me alone for good. Mama said there were more fish in the sea, right? Ellis is looking mighty fishy right about now.

Logan steps in between us.

"Ellis, will you excuse us a minute?"

Ellis looks from me to Logan.

"You want me to leave you two alone?" He directs the question over to me.

"Not really. What were those classes again?" I step around Logan to get a better view of the ledger in Ellis' hand.

"Sociology and Algebra Two." He points to them as he says it.

"Algebra Two? You must be really good at math. I'm going to need lots of tutoring," I say. If Logan isn't writhing from the daggers I'm churning, I'm pretty sure I'm not the fish for him.

"Are you done?" Logan pushes into Ellis with his shoulder. It's like he's gone animal, which reminds me of that roar. His kisses stream through my mind like a slideshow, causing my stomach to bottom out like I'm on a roller coaster.

"Enough." I bite the air with my anger. "I'll talk to you." I turn to Ellis. "Thank you. I look forward to your help," I whisper.

"For the record," Logan whispers as Ellis leaves, "I tutored him in math two years in a row."

"Like I said, you're a real superhero. So how long before you get your girlfriend's diary back? A week? A month? Next two years? I really don't want your excuses."

"I'm not giving excuses." He shifts from one foot to the other. "I checked the schedule. You know how many classes we have together?"

"You and me, or you and Michelle?" Honestly, I don't know anymore.

"You and me." He looks like a statue of perfection in this light. He's so gorgeous it hurts.

A hot spear of raw attraction bisects my abdomen.

"How many?" I'm hoping for at least three.

"None." A genuine look of disappointment sweeps across his face.

"None?" I say, trying not to sound too alarmed.

"What are the odds, right?"

"I don't know." I'm perfectly stunned. "What about lunch?"

"You have B, I have A."

"Lovely." Then I start to panic about Brielle and what about Michelle? Will she be dining with Logan? I don't like this. I don't like this at all. "I'd better get up there." A huge knot lodges in the center of my throat. I pull a pen and paper from my purse, ignoring the ones laid out and head over to the boards until I find my name. As I jot down my classes it occurs to me that both Ellis and Logan had to have checked their classes and compared them to mine. I'm not so surprised Logan did it, but Ellis? Interesting.

I take my list and look down at the O's. I find Logan and Gage together like usual. Logan's right—nothing together. I compare my classes with the ones Gage is registered for. English Lit, Algebra Two, World History, I scan down the list. All the same classes. All the same times.

I try to find him in the crowd.

"Boo," he says, standing square in front of me.

"Did you do this?" I hold out my schedule accusingly.

"No, I didn't do this, technically a computer network did. But it's pretty cool." His eyes laser through mine, and for a minute I'm right back in that truck again, melting away like delicious warm chocolate.

Michelle comes in with Emily and Lexy, and the three of them make a beeline over to Logan. Michelle doesn't waste any time snatching his schedule from out of his hands and comparing notes. She nods approvingly. Her hand flies up, and he meets it with a high five.

I'm not sure what Logan doesn't get about the way I feel when I see the two of them together—how it feels like someone set your clothes on fire and refuses to help put them out.

I rake my hand through Gage's hair.

"Yeah. It's pretty cool."

35

Burn

Outside the dark sky boils as it seals in the last hot spell of summer. A light pepper of rain falls, refreshing us in this oppressive heat.

Drake wants to stop for lunch at the bowling alley in hopes to see Brielle, and since Mom and Tad have put him in charge of my whereabouts today, I don't really have a say in the matter. Tad assumed Drake wouldn't lose me. I wanted to inform him Drake was very responsible with me the night before, but I bit my tongue. Besides, Mia and Melissa were sitting right there. I don't want to give them any ideas about sneaking out in the middle of the night.

The air conditioning is on full blast in the bowling alley. It feels amazing in contrast to the hot sticky climate percolating outside.

Gage insists on giving me a tour of the kitchen. Large stainless appliances line the back wall. A long center island cluttered with bowls and utensils is bustling with a pair of busy workers preparing the orders streaming in.

He leads me over to a large metal door, and a white fog billows out when he opens it.

"Walk-in freezer. Hang out in there a few minutes and it'll really cool you off."

"Can you get locked in?" I'd be afraid to work here for that reason alone.

"Nope." He slides his hand up and down the smooth inside of the door. "Shuts just like a refrigerator."

Logan comes back and walks past us as he pulls down a giant sleeve of hotdog buns.

"Are you ready to work for me?" His brows twitch in a flirtatious manner. Logan's eyes are the most amazing amber color I've ever seen. There's something wild about them, almost primitive. I'm fascinated by how they glow.

"Maybe I will. I think I'd enjoy working with Gage," I say, just to piss him off.

His expression sours.

"Him I'm about to fire," he remarks, taking his bag and heading back into the kitchen.

"You guys usually get along?" I have a feeling the riff is a new thing, and it's all my fault.

"We've fought before." Gage leans into the kitchen with a dark expression.

"Over Chloe?"

His lips pull into a line.

I don't know Gage as well as Logan, but it seems to me in a lot of ways they're opposites. I'm starting to wonder if Gage is better boyfriend material than Logan. Gage told me he'd never do the things Logan was doing.

"Why does Michelle have Chloe's diary anyway?" I pull back and spy on Logan as he works the food line. You'd never know he runs this place. He's right in the mix with the rest of the employees pulling all the hard jobs, not bossing anyone around. Brielle's forever telling me she loves working here.

"She says her mother gave her a box of Chloe's things. She found it."

"I bet she read it cover to cover."

"You'd think."

"So were you and Chloe pretty close?"

"We went out a few times." He socks his fist softly into a metal shelving unit.

A loud hiss comes from the corner of the kitchen and the noxious odor of burning tortilla chips permeates the air.

Gage bolts back into the kitchen and attempts to put a lid over the fryer, but a tornado of flames shoots up out of it and runs halfway across the ceiling.

"Skyla!" Logan shouts from the other side of the counter. He jumps through the service window and rushes over to where I'm standing, frozen.

The kitchen drains of employees as Logan commands them out. I turn to move and knock something solid over with my foot causing a gush of liquid to rush around my feet.

"Get out now!" Gage shouts as he struggles to pull me in his direction.

In nothing more than a quiet whisper, the floor ignites in flames. Tall spears of fire separate me from Gage. An entire barricade forms and a huge rushing wall erupts between Logan and me.

I try to move, but it feels like my tennis shoes are being suctioned to the ground. The first air-brained thought that whizzes through my mind is that I must have stepped in gum. I lift my shoes and it looks more like I stepped in a pile of marshmallow fluff, only what's really happening is the cheap tennis shoes my mother bought are melting right off my feet.

"Help!" I choke out the word. A dense smoke fills the kitchen. A loud blowing noise drills in my ear. It forces the flames down, extinguishing them into a sea of white clouds.

My eyes seal shut from the smoke. An arm reaches under my knees and lifts me off the ground. I push my face into the shirt of whoever has me and desperately try gasping for breath. We move outside in a fury. I take in the fresh air, choking out what's left of the smoke.

"You're OK." A kiss drops down on the top of my head. It's Logan's voice I hear.

"Logan!" I circle my arms around the back of his neck. "What just happened?"

"I don't know. We've never had anything like that before."

"Skyla." Gage walks up gasping for air. His face is blackened from soot illuminating his eyes like twin beacons. "You OK?"

Logan replaces me on the ground causing my shoes to stick unnaturally.

"I'm fine." I try to dust off the soot from my jeans only to smear it into long black streaks.

The shrill cry of a siren drills through the air.

"I checked the temp, and the oil was fine." Gage gives a quizzical look. "Do you think?" He doesn't finish his thought.

"I know," Logan breathes the word.

The two of them lock eyes in an immovable gaze.

"What?" I yell. "This involves me. I was in that fire."

"Fire is the only sure way to kill a Celestra," Gage says.

"Fire?" My father died in a fire.

Logan opens his mouth then shuts it as Brielle dives in on top, blanketing me with a hug.

"I can't believe you survived! They made us run out the back. I had no idea you guys were standing out here. The entire kitchen is destroyed."

"I'm sorry." I direct it at Logan. It's because of me. Whatever it was, it wanted me.

36

Smash

Mom and Tad are frantic when they pick me up from the emergency room. The doctor on duty assured them I had no signs of damage to my lungs, and my blood oxygen level was perfectly normal.

After I shower and dress, my mother makes me lie down in the family room where she covers me with a blanket and makes me try to eat disgusting day glow yellow chicken soup from powder and drink bland tea.

"I almost burned to death. I don't have diarrhea." I'm quick to remind her as she ups the ante and offers to make me toast.

She holds her hands up near her temples and shudders.

"I can't lose you Skyla. Too much has already happened here. I'm starting to think moving was a very big mistake."

I toss the covers off. It's stifling in the house, and her last comment sends a heated rush of adrenaline through me.

"I think moving here was the best thing that's happened to this family in a really long time." Like before Dad, but I don't say that part.

"You think the best thing about moving here is named, Logan," she says his name like it's the plague.

"I'm sure there are boys named Logan everywhere." I try to appease her by making it sound as though I could have fallen for someone anywhere, but deep down inside I don't believe a word. "You met Tad at work." I shrug. They both worked for the same design firm in L.A. The way Tad whooped about opening his own division on Paragon you'd think he won the lottery. I think my mom assumed she'd be an equal partner, but from what I've seen, she's nothing more than his secretary.

Tad walks by and breezes into the kitchen. We watch together as he inventories the refrigerator then slams it shut with disappointment.

"Lizbeth, there's no food in this damn house." He says it in such a comical way I think he's half joking. Who talks to my mother that way? My dad would shoot him if he could. He'd probably want me to do it for him. Sure my mom and he fought, but he never addressed her that way, at least never around me.

In less than ten minutes my mom and the Gestapo are doing a grocery run. Unfreakingbelievable.

Drake and the girls are quiet upstairs so I head on up to grab my phone so I can chat with Logan. My jealous rage toward Michelle seems to have subsided for the moment. I mean he did pull me out of a burning building. He did kill a Fem for me. And then there's Gage who lifted Logan's truck out of the way of oncoming traffic.

A cold chill descends upon me as I climb the stairs. I rub my bare arms running up the final steps. It's freezing up here. Drake's door is shut and so is the girls. The hall window is fixed so it can't be coming from there. I lay my hand across the glass, warm like the weather outside. So where's this cold air coming from? Neither the heating nor the AC works in this place. I have a feeling the blue light special had a little more to do with this defunct lemon and all of the broken amenities, than it did the disappearance of one of its residents or any so called ghosts.

The air continues to become more frigid as I move down the hall. I bypass my bedroom with my hands extended before me like a zombie.

"Oh my gosh," I whisper in disbelief. A light fog fills the hole of my parent's bedroom. I walk in, treading with caution. It looks remarkably normal. The comforter is drawn tight over the bed, and a hundred microscopic pillows sit neatly arranged in rows. "Please, God, kill me if I ever live like this."

I head in a little deeper into the heart of the sharp, glacial chill. It's so cold it stings my flesh like a sunburn.

"What is this?" I ask out loud as though I might get some sort of answer.

The door to the closet is open. I'm immediately attracted in a morbid way to the dark gaping hole. It's an icebox in here. You could hang meat. I pull the string dangling from the center of the walk-in and turn on the light. My mother and Tad have divided the closet down the middle. My mom's clothes are arranged in no special order with the exception of long dresses toward the left, but Tad's side reeks of anal. Dress shirts are scaled from black to white in color order. Who does that? Maybe a girl would do that—maybe a thirteen-year-old girl would color code her wardrobe, but a grown man? His pants are laid out the same way, even his shoes fan out in a depressed rainbow of color.

An icy bite of air circles around my left leg. It's as though it's speaking to me, telling me something. I crouch down and feel with my hand until I hit the back wall behind Tad's shoes. It's dripping wet. My fingers snag on a small lever. I pull it down opening a small door in the wall. I pat my hand around blindly and come up with a stack of paper.

I riffle through it, and my heart feels like it's going to seize up, not to mention this piercing cold air has me feeling lightheaded.

A stack of hundred dollar bills—fifty, hundred dollar bills.

Shit! I never want to hear him harp about not having two dimes to rub together, again. The next time he does this, I might just say, *no dipshit—we have Benjamin's.*

A waddle of newspaper clippings wrapped in a rubber band vies for my attention. I go to loosen the band, severing it accidentally.

Great.

I open them up and flatten them out with the palm of my hand.

A bunch of these are about Dad's accident. The other three are clippings of a missing West Paragon High School girl. Chloe. Another one from last October, about this house being haunted.

I scramble putting everything back together the way I found it and shut it back in the tiny compartment.

I get up and start heading out of the room and run smack into Tad himself.

37

Secrets

"Get a small bottle or plastic bag and collect some of the moisture," Logan instructs me over the phone.

I consider this a moment. Perhaps calling Logan with the odd news of what I discovered on Tad's side of the closet wasn't the best idea. Plus I had a mild heart attack when Tad walked back in to get his wallet. I told him I was just borrowing Mom's hairspray and he didn't bat a lash.

"You don't get it," I say. "The clippings were just weird. He's psycho! I'm living with a lunatic."

"I agree with you. The clippings are strange. But Skyla, listen to me—go right now and find something to capture that moisture. I'll give it to my uncle, and he'll analyze it."

"Analyze it? It's water."

"It may be something more than that."

"Like ghost water?" OK, that made no sense.

He expels a heavy sigh into the phone.

"I'm sorry," I whisper.

"You did nothing wrong. Listen, I'm coming over."

"You can't come over. My parents will kill me." And it kills me that I just referred to Mom and Tad collectively as, my parents.

The line goes dead.

Logan arrives seemingly on foot. He parked somewhere below Brielle's driveway and appeared at the backdoor of the kitchen.

I give a small yelp when I see him waving. My hand flies up to my throat as I jump backward into the sink.

"You know I'm afraid to look out this door," I scold as I let him in. Mia and Melissa are in the back practicing how to play spin the bottle for a party they've been invited to. I'll have to teach them later how to manipulate it just perfectly, so the bottle lands square on the boy you want to kiss.

Logan and I head upstairs. He pulls a small glass vial from his pocket just like the one he took my blood in.

"You get a bulk discount on those?" I say sarcastically.

"With you around I might have to." He gives a slight grin.

I take him straight into my parent's closet, turn on the light and orient him to the exact area. It's not so unearthly cold in here anymore. Before I can ask if it's good. I hear my mother shout from the bottom of the stairs.

"Help unload the car please!" Her voice carries up the stairs.

Without thinking, I bolt out of the room and head downstairs in an effort to keep them from heading up. It would have been nice if I informed Logan of my plan. But he's a bright boy. He'll figure it out.

"Don't just stand there like a statue. Get out there and grab some groceries," Tad barks as he heads through the door.

A part of me wants to listen and run out to the minivan, but it's parked so far away, and by the time I get back Tad might already be upstairs changing.

Mia and Melissa each come in with an armful of bags. Funny, I don't see Drake in the familial equation. He's probably upstairs with Brielle, bathing, or playing hide-and-seek, or whatever the hell it is they do. Drake is clearly the golden child who can do no wrong.

"Hey, young lady." Tad snaps his finger toward the van.

"Oh God," I mouth as I sprint down to the open trunk and grab the last of the paper bags. I make a mad dash up the porch and spill half the contents of a bag full of loose fruit. Who puts loose fruit in a paper bag?

I run the bags to the entry and place them on the floor in an effort to bolt back and gather the rolling apples and pears. I spot a bunch of bananas that have managed to fall under the slotted stairs. Shit! It's going to take an entire millennium to scurry up the slope and retrieve them. I decide to ignore them and head inside.

I unload my bags onto the kitchen counter as Mom and Tad bitch about the lousy job the guy at the grocery store did of bagging up their stuff. Little do they know there are much bigger things to bitch about such as the boy I left stranded in their bedroom. I toss the fruit in a glass bowl mom has set out with a few heavily puckered apples already in it.

I fold the paper bags neatly and put them away, then stretch my hands out and yawn dramatically.

"I think I'll catch a nap."

"And where the hell are the bananas? I know I put them in the cart," Tad complains as they both ignore my spontaneous monologue.

I take the stairs two by two and head straight into their bedroom. It's not cold anymore. In fact the air is stuffy and stale like it usually is in here. I whip open their closet.

"Logan?" I hiss.

Nothing.

I take a peek in their bathroom, and that's when Mom and Tad decide to walk in. He's got his hands cupping both her breasts outside her shirt, and she's laughing like she actually enjoys that perv touching her.

It's a real deer in the headlights moment, with Tad's hands dropping straight to his side as the expression falls right off Mom's face. A small bit of vomit rises to the back of my throat.

"Just borrowing the hairspray," I say, afraid the image will engrave itself in my brain as I walk past them.

Too late—already has.

38

Passage

He couldn't have left, I would have seen him—someone would have seen him.

I lock my bedroom door. It looks as though there's a body underneath my covers, but then again it always looks like that because I never make my bed.

"Psst?" I hiss walking carefully as though he might pop out at me. "Logan?"

A small sliver of light emerges from the line under my closet door, and I head on over.

I find Logan inside sitting Indian style, reading a book. Everything about him is perfectly serene. You could easily exchange the surroundings for a library, and he would fit right in.

"You should really consider putting a nice comfy chair in here. It's a great place to take your mind off things and relax." He tosses the book behind him. "Maybe a bean bag?"

"Funny." I slide a pile of shoes to the side with my foot. "How are we going to get you out?" I well up with fear at the prospect of Logan becoming forever trapped in my closet.

"   't worry." He hits the air brakes with his hand. "I'm   bring sustenance when needed. And we can do *this*."

He pulls me down over him and presses in with a long searing kiss. "I want to show you something."

"What?" I rub the palms of my hands across his chest in a series of small circles. The scent of laundry softener lights up my senses.

"Not that, but it's a good idea for later." He pulls us both to our feet. "Up there." He points to the top shelf toward the back. "You have a chair we can stand on?"

I haul in the rolling desk chair that glides around like it's on ice.

"I'll hold it," I offer.

Logan climbs on and reaches up toward the wall. His feet engage in a full swivel in both directions as my fingers slip off the back.

"Oops sorry," I say.

"There might only be two of us left, Skyla. Please don't try to kill me."

"Really, are there only two of us left?" If we were the last of the Celestra then it would be our genetic duty to produce offspring—lots and lots of offspring.

"No, but at the rate they're killing us, we might get there soon." Something snaps, and the wall comes off in his hand.

"It's a façade!" I don't know why this thrills me.

"Most things are." He hands it down to me, and I place it upright between my winter jackets. A sliding panel door bumps back, and there's a two and a half foot wide opening. "Come on." He urges me to climb up there.

"What is it, the attic?" I take his hands and let him help me up into the narrow dark opening.

"It's," he grunts as he pushes himself in after me. "It's a locked off portion of it. Chloe didn't know it was there until just a few months before she... discovered it by accident."

"Oh." A pinch of jealousy stirs hot inside me. "Were you trapped in her bedroom and in need of a way out?"

He doesn't bother with a laugh. Instead he gropes around above me and a small bare bulb goes off.

I suck in a lungful of air. It's beautiful. The walls are covered in a million paper butterflies—large, small, every color of the rainbow. It must have taken her hours, weeks, maybe even months to fill in all the bare spaces.

"This was her getaway. I was here once, and that was because she kept something I gave her, here."

"You came to check on it?" I can't help but bite into him a little each time he mentions her. I guess I am the jealous type, and I don't really care if he knows it.

"I came to get it back." His eyebrows give a gentle rise.

"So you have it?" I don't even know what *it* is, but I love the fact it was something akin to the breakup collection agency more than it was a secret rendezvous.

"No she never gave it back." His gaze wanders past the wall into oblivion, reliving the moment.

"What was it?"

"A pendant that belonged to my grandmother. Chloe said she wanted to give it back. And then she went missing and that was that."

"I thought you said she let you in here, and she was going to give it to you?"

"I never said that. I said I've only been here once. It was after she was gone. Brielle took me up here when I told her Chloe had something important of mine."

"Oh. Maybe she was wearing it—you know, when they took her."

"She wore it for a little while, then she wanted to prove she didn't need it. We had a fight and I never saw her wear it again. She told Brielle she was keeping it in her diary."

"Strange place to keep jewelry." My eyes narrow in on him. "Maybe she got rid of it or pawned it. Do you believe her?"

"She couldn't lie to me," he says serious.

Of course she could lie to him. Anybody can lie to anybody. It's part of the rules of this game called life. Not that it feels good or it's right or that anybody should do it, but it is possible. It's like he thinks she was perfect. He has a serious case of a Chloe-based messiah complex.

"She could lie." I match his over serious tone to the T. It's comical, both of us here in a paper butterfly sanctuary created by his dead ex-girlfriend, having a spat over, of all things, the virtues of his ex.

"I think I like you jealous." His lips curve into a delicious smile. He leans in and bites gently on my lower lip causing a full-blown meltdown in my stomach. We spend the better part of an hour making good use of the gorgeous surroundings—the inflexible sturdy floor. I don't think I could ever stay mad at Logan.

A hard thump comes from below. I can hear my mother muffling something through the door.

"Just a minute," I shout. "I have to go." I hop back down into the closet.

"I'm leaving," Logan whispers, hitching his thumb behind him.

I don't ask questions, just throw a whole mess of clothes up there and pretend the butterfly room never existed.

39

Lost

I wait until well after dinner, when my mom and Tad retire to their bedroom to do whatever freaky things it is they do back there, before barricading myself in my room. I not only take the routine precautions of locking the door, I slide the dresser against it to ensure no one will dare try to pound their way in. Next, I turn on the shower and let the water run in the event someone should come bang away, they might hear the water and figure I'm indisposed.

I don't know what excites me so much about having a secret passage in my bedroom. My room is easily a hundred times the size of the tiny space embellished with butterflies, so it must be the secrecy of it all. I climb in just barely able to pull myself up on the shelf. I definitely need more upper body strength. Maybe this could be a weight room or something? I could do yoga or pilates. Then again the lack of fresh air and circulation might become an issue, already it's so dank and muggy up here.

I flick on the light and drag up a spare throw pillow I plucked from off my bed and take a seat on it. Even the floor is unique, made of some kind of soft black vinyl, speckled with silver flecks. It feels like I'm sitting on stars, like I have the entire galaxy at my feet.

I pick on a loose thread on the side of the pillow. I'm getting so sleepy. It's been such a long day.

I shift and lie down. It's so easy to relax up here. I close my eyes and drift off to sleep.

When I wake up, I have this weird feeling in my brain like someone opened my skull and poured in a can of soda. Carbonated—it feels carbonated.

The light is off, which panics me into reaching for the pull cord, and thankfully it illuminates the cozy room once again. I turn to leave out the crawl space, and the exit is blocked.

Shit! I've been sealed in, probably by Tad.

I fudge it a little, and it slides right open, but the façade is back on.

"What the?" I push it out and it falls to the floor with a whimper. Besides, I pushed a five hundred pound dresser over the door and...wait—the water's off.

I head out of the closet, and immediately notice the furniture's been reconfigured. A brass bed sits where my bed was last, but it's not mine, and neither is the dresser or the rug or the desk—or the girl sitting at the desk!

I slap my hand over my mouth.

Don't panic—I plead with myself as I step back into the closet. She's got her ear-buds in and she's spinning a pencil between her fingers.

It must be Chloe. It is Chloe. I recognize her from the pictures, the dreams. That must mean...oh, God, no. I can't time travel. I don't know the rules. What if I'm stuck here forever? Technically I already am here, safely tucked in L.A. And if it's over two years ago, so is dad. I could catch a flight and go home and save him. I could be my own long lost twin or something.

I peek back out into the room. Her cell must have gone off because she picks it up and starts speaking into it.

Wait a minute...if she's talking, why can't I hear her? Oh my gosh. I'm broken.

A rush of panic flushes through me. I try to will myself to hear. Logan said all the gifts could be learned, but I had to believe—no doubt allowed. I can do this. I can hear Chloe.

I peer back out in the room at her. Great she's laughing.

I squeeze my eyes shut and repeat, *I can hear her right now.* Over and over again until something pops in the atmosphere and I hear a cackle come from outside the door.

"You think I care what kind of car you drive? You could ride a bike, and I wouldn't care," she purrs into the phone. "Get white."

White? As in a truck?

"Tell him to get black, silver is way too close."

She's bossing them both around. I shake my head in disbelief.

"I can't. I have practice. But I'll take a rain check. If I make tryouts I'll let you buy me something nice." She laughs again. "And if you make varsity, I'll buy you something nice." She laughs. "Me? I'm partial to jewels. *Family* jewels." The sound of her chortling makes me wish I were deaf again.

She was joking. She threw in some stupid double entendre, and he gave her his grandmother's pendant. And where did she put it? Her dumb diary.

I go to climb back on the chair and there isn't one.

No chair!

Chloe passes right by me and I straighten stiff as a board against the frame of her closet—er, my closet. Whatever.

I hear the bathroom door shut. Impulsively, I dash out and snatch the chair from beneath her desk, which is ten times as heavy as the one I own, probably because her mother insists on buying something of quality and not succumbing to the ultra thrifty ways of her miserly new husband.

A silver sparkle catches my eye, and I pause on my way back to the closet. A round filigree pendant with a cut blue stone in the middle sits off to the side of her notebook.

He's already given it to her. I reach over and pick it up. It's so heavy.

The toilet flushes.

I tuck the pendant in my jeans and hightail it back to the closet with the chair. It takes me less than ten seconds to hop back in the hole and into the butterfly room.

Now what?

I start plucking at the butterflies while tears of frustration burn behind my lids.

Maybe I just need to sleep?

40

Found

My eyes flutter open. There's a hand on my shoulder shaking me, and for a minute I think it's Mom, and that I'm in my own bed.

"Five more minutes." As the words slip out of my mouth I can sense the stifled acoustic of my own voice smothering in the tiny space.

I bolt up and scoot back. I hit the wall so hard it feels like the pins holding up the butterflies have pressed through my flesh, and I let out a yelp.

"Shh!" She brings her finger up over her mouth as her eyes narrow in on me, hard. "Who are you?"

She doesn't seem at all alarmed—annoyed, yes, alarmed, no.

"Skyla."

"Skyla?" She turns her head to get a better look at me as her expression dims. "And you're from the past or the future?" She looks down as though she's about to rip my throat out.

"How did you know?" I soften a bit. At least I don't think she's going to call the cops or kill me for sport.

"Doesn't matter." She fills her lungs with a hopeless breath. "Which one?" She seems more than curious, like it matters on a larger scale than I can comprehend.

"Future."

She gives a hard blink. Chloe isn't at all harsh and bitchy like I had imagined her. In fact she's, I hate to say it—pretty nice.

"So I guess something happens to me." She puts her fingers in her mouth and starts chewing her nails.

"Oh you shouldn't do that it's a hotbed of germs, plus guys hate it." Wait a minute why am I giving her advice on guys? She's dating my hot boyfriend as we speak.

"Stop. I'm probably dead anyway. What did you come for?"

I take that back, slight bitch.

"I didn't come for anything. This is my room now, and I just found out about this, this..." I wave my hands around. "Whatever you call it."

"Oh." She takes it better than I thought. "So you don't know how to use it."

"Time travel? Are you..." I squint my eyes at her.

"I'm an angel." She nods. "And it's no coincidence you're in my room. I bet you have my friends, my..." She lets the thought dangle not wanting to complete it. "Not that it's important. Look, you wouldn't be here unless you wanted something. What is it?" She snaps.

I shake my head incredulously. Then a light goes off in my brain. I dig into my pocket and pull out the pendant.

"I want this."

"You bitch!" She snatches it back.

"I wasn't trying to steal it. You flushed the toilet, and I needed to get back up here and plus..." I bite down on my bottom lip.

"Plus what?" Her lips blacken unnaturally.

"Plus..." I close my eyes a second. I really pray I'm not going to regret this. "Logan is searching for it."

Her head picks up a notch as though she just noticed me, as though everything I had said before was blather, and now I had finally said the one thing she wanted to hear, or was afraid to.

"Well I'm not giving it to you." She presses it against her chest. "How do I know you're going to give it to him?"

"I swear." I cross my heart and hold out my fingers.

"I'll hold onto it, thank you very much."

"Keep it in your diary." It speeds out of me. I can't believe this—it was my stupid idea.

"My diary? Who puts jewelry in their diary? What am I suppose to do? Notch out a hole like some common criminal?" She looks at me incredulous.

"Yes!" I touch my nose and point at her simultaneously. "And when you do that, be sure and put your diary in this room."

She shakes her head vigorously.

"Why?"

"Brielle knows all about this room. I don't want her reading it. And I don't want you or anybody else reading it either." She pulls back and inspects me.

"Michelle will. She's the one who's going to end up with it if you don't hide it up here where no one will find it. She'll give it to Logan and he'll read it too." I'm not making any promises. I might read it. I *will* read it.

Her head shoots back an inch with surprise.

"Logan can't read it."

"Personally, I don't understand why you don't just burn the darn thing and leave the pendant on the floor."

A choking sound gets locked in her throat. She clutches softly at her neck, and tears well up in her eyes.

"It's all that will be left of me. All my thoughts, all my dreams—ideas, a detailed list of people I hate." She ticks her head to the side and shrugs. "No." It comes out firm. "I can't destroy it, but you have to swear to me you won't read a word, or I will come back, and I will haunt you, and you will wish very badly that we never had this conversation." Her finger sticks in my chest matching the intensity of the pins in my back.

"Done."

She inhales sharply before bringing her hands to her hips. Reaching behind her she plucks at the smallest turquoise butterfly nestled in a bed of red makeshift flowers and plucks at it until a tiny door opens. Its pitch black in there, looks like it's flocked or lined with felt. A few books and a small box lie stacked on top of one another causing me to look away quickly because I don't want to snoop. Plus, I can always snoop later when she's not around.

"It'll be in here. I'll put the pendant in the diary, and remember you can't read a word."

"OK. So how do I get back?" I rub my sweaty palms down over my jeans.

"Easy. I'll send you." A manufactured grin spreads wide across her face. She makes a fist and pulls back. I see it coming, and I still don't believe she's going to hit me, then—

41

Mine

My eyes flutter open and I think I'm in bed, but the mattress is hard as a rock, and I remember exactly where I am as I sit straight up. The side of my face throbs and I pat the swollen flesh with my fingertips.

The passage door is open. I look down, and I see my chair and recognize my clothes and hear the shower water running. I'm so emotional I feel like sobbing.

The tiny turquoise butterfly catches my attention. I gently pull the knob like I saw Chloe do, and the door pops right open. It's there. A fat book with bloated pages sits on top of the wooden jewelry box along with the same stack of books as I saw earlier. I hold the book to my chest and close the door to the secret compartment.

Out in my room, safe on my bed, I keep it curled to my chest for a good long while as silent tears stream their way down my cheek. What must she have thought when I left? Did knowing she was going to die take the fight out of her? What if I told her she was going to be tortured? Or that they would bury her body in a shallow grave at the bottom of Devil's Peak? Would it have made a difference? Or what if she knew I was in love with her boyfriend? I wonder if she thought I was pretty?

OK, that last thought was completely uncalled for. I wipe the tears from my eyes and start in on the diary. It opens to the dead middle and there's something wrong. I shag the book out over my bed. She glued the pages along the periphery of the entire text. The only way I'd be able to read this is if I had an X-Acto knife—very clever.

A small portion near the bottom is taped up and I can feel the pendant underneath. I tear it out from the thin veil of wrapping and caress it in between my fingers. Heavy— the stone is soft as butter. I bring it up to my lips and rub it over them until I can feel it, even when it's not there. It's beautiful. It must mean something though. What kind of value could it have that Logan is willing to move heaven and earth to get it? Just because it was his grandmother's? I don't think so. I get the feeling it's something more.

I have to go to cheer practice. I have to.

I love that there is one thing in my life that neither my mother nor Tad can give me grief over.

Michelle, Emily and Lexy are fashionably late, so I hightail it over to the football field and flag down Logan.

He comes over pulling off his helmet, beads of sweat dripping down the sides of his face. He squints into a smile and leans in to kiss me.

Logan Oliver is hot—literally and physically.

"Something spectacular happened last night." OK, that was a little more dramatic than I intended, but still.

"You found another room?" He teases.

"No. Is there one?"

He runs his fingers through the back of my hair. "No," he whispers with a little laugh. "Actually I don't have any idea. What was so spectacular?"

"Time travel!" I beam up at him.

The coach whistles over at Logan.

"I gotta go. Don't ever joke like that. If you come in contact with someone, it could change things." He presses in a quick kiss. "You could hasten someone's death if you're not careful."

I watch as he runs back to the field.

I don't know if I killed her, but I'm sure I took the fight out of her.

I wait until Mom and Tad go to bed. I place the dresser back over my door and turn on the shower. I climb into the butterfly room and arrange the four pillows I've dragged up here. Clutching at Chloe's diary, I try my hardest to fall asleep. It's funny how sleep doesn't come when you want it—how it wants to hang out far too long when you no longer need it.

I can feel the passage of time. My lids flutter as I struggle to open them. I take in a deep breath of stifling air and sit up. The cover is back over the opening! I'm back.

I open the door to the passage extra careful not to scare her into having a heart attack or inspire her to throw a ninja star at me or something equally stupid, but deadly.

I can't make out any noise, so I take a second to convince myself that I can hear. My ears fill with the sound of rushing water, then stabilize. I hop down and move to the edge of the closet. I see her out there with her ear-buds in, threading a pencil through her fingers.

Same day. I think.

She picks up her cell and plucks out an ear-bud.

The diary in my hand starts to shiver. It warms beneath my fingers then evaporates into nothing.

I did it. Chloe will never know I was here, and she can fight for her life. But what if she survives? I'll be somewhere else. I might even still be on Paragon. Surely there's another cursed house that no one wants to touch with a ten-foot pole that Tad can get at cost, right? But what if there's not, and I never see Logan again?

"You think I care what kind of car you drive? You could ride a bike and I wouldn't care." She purrs into the phone. "Get white."

Logan's right there on the other line. Maybe while she's in the bathroom I can call him back and give him my number?

I express my disappointment in one quick breath.

"Tell him to get black, silver is way too close."

Get on with it.

"I can't. I have practice. But I'll take a rain check. If I make tryouts I'll let you buy me something nice." She laughs again.

"And if you make varsity, I'll buy you something nice." She laughs "Me? I'm partial to jewels. *Family* jewels."

Yes we know.

She walks passed me and heads into the bathroom. I speed over and start dragging the chair back. The pendant catches my eye again. It's so pretty. Unique.

I look over my shoulder at the open mouth of the closet. People misplace things all the time. And Logan will thank me for it, plus no more Michelle.

I snake it off the dresser and stuff it into my jeans.

The toilet flushes.

I make a beeline to the butterfly room. I believe if I don't fall asleep Chloe will come in and beat me. I can sleep. I can...

42

Yours

It worked! I hug all four of my pillows at once then hop back down to my bedroom. I pluck the pendant out of my pocket and kiss it with a squeal of delight.

This time I didn't speak to Chloe, so she'll have no clue what her future holds. A thick feeling of guilt coats me from the inside. I should have warned her. I should find out where this horrible thing happens and help her circumvent it.

I should also go back to my old life in L.A. and tell my old self all about this cool guy named Logan and how I have to force my mother to buy a house on Paragon...except one tiny detail, I don't know how to get anywhere. And the simple fact I'm back in my own bedroom means that returning the diary and staying out of Chloe's life, still yielded the same deadly results.

The pendant warms in my hand. At least I can give it back to Logan, and it's good-bye Michelle.

I pick my cell up off my desk and flop on my bed.

I have something you want ~S

Less than ten seconds later.

Are you in the mood to give it away?

What? No! But yes!!! ~S

He'll never guess in a million years I have the pendant. I'll just tell him I found it in the secret compartment in the butterfly room.

Can you come over? ~S

Sorry.

Why not ~S

It takes a little longer than I like for him to get back to me.

I'm with M. @ the movies. She's in the bathroom and I SWEAR this ends tonight.

I don't text him back.

Later, in my angry dreams, I think I see Michelle. She laughs at me while waving Logan's sweater like a flag.

Something soft and wet trails my neck and I struggle to wake up, trying to shoo the dog away. Then I remember with perfect clarity we don't have a dog and I shoot out of bed like a pistol.

It's Logan holding his hands up in the surrender position. He's got a remorseful grin on his face and something rectangular tucked under his arm. He plucks it out and holds up the diary victoriously.

"You got it!" I say far too loud. I slap my hand over my mouth and motion for Logan to help me move the dresser against my door.

Once we finish, he passes me the diary.

"You read it?" I whisper.

"Not yet."

It's still bound with glue. Each page is petrified together, you can't read it or add another entry—that means Michelle didn't read it either.

I exhale hard. A lump forms in my throat. I know she's been gone almost a year, but I saw her. I was just with her, twice this week.

I pluck the pendent out of my pocket and go to hide it in the palm of my hand, but the rough corner of it pricks me.

"Ouch!" The pendent ejects out of my hand and dances across the floor.

"You found it." There's a note of exceptional wonder in his voice. He picks it up off the floor and holds it out like an exotic specimen. "Where'd you find it?" He doesn't take his eyes off it.

"I didn't." I meant to say, *the butterfly room.* I bring my fingers up over my lips.

"You took it?" He looks puzzled. "Time travel." His face drains of all color.

It becomes quickly apparent that I've somehow botched things again.

"People lose things all the time," I say.

"Not things they need to eat, and breathe, and see."

"What are you talking about?"

"It's a protective hedge." He flips it in the air like a coin. A great look of sadness comes over him. "I wondered why she took it off. Why she put it in her diary of all places."

I swallow hard. Chloe must have remembered something from my first visit. Clearly I have no clue about time travel.

"Here." He opens my hand and places it gently down, stone side up. "Wear this. Don't ever take this off. No Sector, or Fem, or Count can kill you. You'll be impervious." He gives a very careful kiss just above my left eyebrow.

Then leaves.

I head back to my bed staring—glaring at the pendant. So I'm the one who took her protective hedge away. I'm the one who turned her loose to an entire hoard of waiting evil. It was me all along.

Logan didn't take her diary. Why were the pages still glued if I undid the first visit? Unless all I did was return the diary. And I'm starting to think I should return the pendant too.

I go over it six ways to Sunday, how I could possibly change things—help Chloe live—find my father and do the same.

I think of the woman hanging from the backdoor, the Fem and its horrid putrefied stench, the men in the wrong way lane, the fire. If I keep the pendant I can avoid an entire lifetime of grief. I could live without having to fear my death—captivity, which is worse than death, and then Gage would be right. I could glide into old age skydiving without a parachute every single day. Or I could do the right thing and give it back.

Tears fill under my lids. I watch the world distort at their command—wobble to and fro—quiver as though it were afraid for its life.

I know what I need to do.

43

Family

Tad and Mom decide since its Melissa's birthday we should all go out to dinner. Melissa votes for the bowling alley, which Tad quickly rejects, and for that I'm thankful. The last thing I want is Tad and my mother near Logan. No thank you.

The Mexican restaurant in downtown Paragon is your traditional villa knockoff with sombreros and colorful paper doilies strewn about on a laundry line. It's dark inside and immediately I like it. It's the exact romantic, exotic environment I imagine Logan and I frequenting. Especially once school starts, since we'll hardly see each other due to our nonexistent classes together. While I'm busy daydreaming about how handsome Logan would be illuminated by one of those small red candles, a pair of hands land flat on my shoulders.

"Hey." It comes in a quick hot whisper.

I pivot around on my heels to find Logan nodding into me with a little more distance than I'm used to.

Gage appears, then his aunt and uncle.

"What are you doing here?" It takes everything in me not to lunge into a hug.

"Hopefully we'll be eating." He tweaks his brows.

"Skyla!" Logan's aunt offers me her hand.

Glancing over I see Mom and Tad bearing down on me with loaded interest. So I introduce them.

My mother is enthralled with Logan's Aunt Emma.

They jab on about textiles and textures, the rustic touch and other irrelevant things until the waitress calls out Melissa's name.

"Why don't you join us?" My mother asks. It sounds so genuine, not obligatory like you would expect it to be.

"Yes!" Emma beams back. "We would love to, right Barron?" He's decidedly less enthused, but agrees. I can see Tad sweating financial bullets already at the thought of paying for an additional four meals.

Logan pulls me back by the elbow as everyone clears the waiting area.

"Where's your pendant?"

"I..." I don't really want to get into it.

"You don't have a chain, do you?" He gives a sly smile and produces a long silver strand from his pocket.

"Excellent." I take it from him nervously. "Wouldn't it be funny if I secretly returned the pendant last night?" I force a giggle.

"It would be very not funny. It couldn't help her now. But *you*, you'll be safe."

"You mean she'd still die?"

"Of course. It doesn't change. Besides, the odds of going back to the exact same place and time are phenomenal. I don't think it could happen."

"So if I had...when I put on the pendant, I'm free of all things scary?" I hold up my hair while he attaches the clasp.

"And nobody will be able to kill you. Ever."

I shut my eyes hard and cry a little over my stupid, stupid mistake.

If I hadn't embarrassed myself before, I was working really hard at it now. You'd think I was at Chloe's funeral the way I pushed my food around my plate and said two words the entire meal. Gage sits on one side of me, and Logan on the other. I feel slightly disoriented and dizzy from all the information Logan just pumped into my brain. If only he would have spelled everything out for me right from the beginning, I would have never gone back on my own volition.

Melissa can't take her eyes off Gage. Its kind of adorable watching an unexpected bit of puppy love bloom, even if it is one sided. We sing to her and she blows out the candle sticking crooked out of the complimentary slice of flan. I'm sure Tad expects us to split it ten ways, so I'm not too stunned when he asks the waitress for extra spoons.

"Melissa, did you make a wish?" Emma asks politely.

"Yes," she's quick to answer. "I wish, when I grow up I marry Gage."

A round of laughter circles the table.

I shake my head, still fogged up in a daze. "Actually, Gage is going to marry *me*." I say matter of fact.

"Skyla!" My mother looks both surprised and miffed. "I thought you were seeing Logan?"

"I am. It's twisted."

When the check comes, Logan's Uncle Barron insists on treating the birthday girl and covers the entire bill.

Everyone rises to their feet simultaneously. Logan shakes Tad's hand then my mother's.

"You mind if I treat Skyla to dessert? I'll bring her home right after." Logan asks still holding her hand in both of his.

"Not at all," she says. "Take your time." She leans into me on the way out. "I like him. Don't blow it."

Typical of my mother, not to have faith in me. What does she think I'm going to do? Burn down his kitchen? Cause a riff between him and his cousin? Return the one gift he gave me that could save my life? All of the above?

The waitress seats us at a table for two, nearby. Logan and I peruse the menu and end up ordering the deep-fried ice cream.

"I can tell my mother loved your parents." My mouth drops as I realize what I've just said. Sure, remind him he's got dead parents. Add it to the list.

"I know what you meant. I consider them my parents. To tell the truth I don't really remember the original set." He pulls a bleak smile.

"I'm sorry. That's terrible." The romantic vision I had is completely destroyed. "She was on the phone with you." I add in a lowered tone. Why not go out with a big bang and upset him over his dead girlfriend, too? "When I saw her, you were picking out a color for your truck."

"Oh," his voice rises as though it were all coming back to him, "and she suggested Gage go with black. He never forgave her for that. It's too hard to keep clean."

It's quiet again. The waitress brings our dessert and two spoons. We start in slow with the task at hand.

"This is really good," I say without emotion.

"I know." He's not eating. He's looking through me with those rare glowing eyes. It's the secret I'm keeping that has him perplexed. He may not know, but he suspects everything.

44

Mystery

At breakfast, Tad announces he's decided to take my mother to the mainland for the day. I'm so thrilled I do a little happy dance underneath the table.

"And I hope all of you behave." He says the last word aimed sarcastically at me.

"I'm not leaving the house. In fact, I'm not even leaving my bedroom." Logan's coming over today. I texted him and asked for a do-over after I fantastically ruined every aspect of last night.

"Great." Tad produces a piece of paper from behind his back. "So you won't have a problem signing this." He lays it flat on the table before me and plops a pen down besides it.

"What's this?" I ask picking it up.

It reads, *I, Skyla Laurel Messenger, pledge not to have wild and out of control parties, or gatherings with two or more people without my parent's full and final consent. I will not have boys over under any circumstance unless both parents approve and at least one parent is present in the company of said boy. I will not drink alcohol, nor will I allow my friends to consume alcohol on my family's property. I will not do illegal drugs, nor smoke cigarettes, cigars, or Salvia. And lastly, I shall not have intimate relations without the bond of marriage while under my parent's roof. If I should choose to become sexually active, I will honor my parent's request and give proof of my selected choice of birth control...*

I jump up from the table. And wave the paper in my mother's face.

"Do you know about this?" I shriek. I knew Tad was sick and twisted, but now he's exposed himself to my mother.

"I do." Her lashes lower and her voice drops to her shoes.

"You do?"

"Yes. I went with him to have it notarized," she adds, a little miffed at my questioning.

"You had this notarized? I can't believe you. You're both sick!" I throw the paper between the two of them.

"You're out of control, Skyla." Tad's calm voice only sets me off even more.

"I'm not out of control. *You're* out of control. You're...you're a freak! A cheap freak! Why do you have a stack of hundred dollar bills locked upstairs in your bedroom?" I clasp my hands on my hips. I'm going to let all the bombs drop and fall where they may. I'm sick of living with this uptight asshole, and when my mother hears what a nutcase he is, she will be, too.

"What are you talking about?" His head rotates in a half circle.

"And what about all those news clippings about this house being haunted, and the dead girl who used to live here?" Both Mia and Melissa let out a shriek. I step into my mother's face. "I bet you didn't know he has a news clipping of Daddy's accident. If that's not grounds for divorce, I don't know what is," I roar.

My mother's head drops down into her chest and hangs there while she tries to absorb it all.

"Lizbeth, what in the hell is your daughter talking about, now?" His face turns purple when he says it, and a vein on his forehead pops from the effort.

"It's mine, Skyla," she groans. "The clippings and the money. They're mine." She lifts her shoulders to her ears.

"Are you hiding money from me? I thought we weren't going to have separate accounts? What happened to what's mine is yours, and what's yours is mine?" He sounds like a child when he says it.

"It is. I swear it is. I like to have a little cash on the side in the event of an emergency. Everybody should have cash at the ready."

"She said there were hundreds of dollars there. How would you feel if I hid hundreds of dollars from you?" He's still changing colors.

"Well the way you don't trust banks, it wouldn't surprise me to find hundreds of dollars inside the mattress!" She yells.

"Why don't you rip it open and find out!" He matches her velocity.

Mia and Melissa are holding each other huddled on the couch, crying, while Drake stands mystified in the hallway.

"What the hell's going on?" he asks.

I pluck the paper off the floor and carry it over to him.

"Here's some light reading for you courtesy of daddy."

Stupid demented document.

I will never forget this.

How my mother can get up and leave with that monkey man stuns me. I let Logan in right through the front door, and lead him up to my bedroom. Both Mia and Melissa are locked in their room due to the high frequency of 'ghost like noises' the house has been experiencing according to them.

I lock the bedroom door behind us and set my comforter on the floor for us to sit on. I have the rug, but I haven't vacuumed since we moved in, and I can hardly stand to walk on it barefoot let alone sit on it with Logan.

He lies flat on his back and lets out a groan.

"Hey, you're not sitting."

"Am I supposed to be sitting?" He glances up at me.

"Yes. It's rule number, five hundred sixty-nine. When a boy enters the house illegally, he must be in a vertical position at all times."

"Does that mean my pants have to be buckled, too?" He gives a loose grin.

"I'll get you a copy of the aforementioned document so you can go over it with your attorney later." I wave it over him like a flag.

"I broke my back on the field today. Is there an exemption for broken backs?"

"Oh yes, it's under the no mercy law. Tad will personally kick you in the balls when you're down, and you'll probably be forced to like it."

"Not funny." He hikes up on his elbows. "I have something you might like though."

"Oh yeah? What's that?" Anything that doesn't have to do with Tad is officially considered good news.

"The results of your blood test are in."

45

Proof

Dr. Barron Oliver, the sign reads, as Logan and I await the test results in his office.

"Sorry for the delay," he says, taking a seat behind the large mahogany desk.

He's got a white lab coat on and a pair of spectacles. He twitches his lips as he silently reads the document shielded by a manila envelope.

Logan and I wait in eager silence of the long coming news. Whatever it says in that report, however much a percent I am Celestra, or even if I have mixed blood, it was a gift from my father. How I wish he could have been here with me, so we could discover our family secrets together. I bet he didn't have any idea about all of the factions and variety of gifts.

"Good news." He looks up at us over his lenses. "First about that moisture sample." He takes off his glasses and bites down on one side. "Unusual amount of plasma." He ticks his head at Logan as though the two of them are speaking some special language.

"What's plasma?" I ask.

"What kind?" Logan taps his hand on the table.

"Plasma is the fundamental liquid component found in blood." Barron says before looking over at Logan. "It was human."

"What the heck is human plasma doing floating around my house? Is my house really haunted?"

"You're a spiritual being, Skyla. Don't you live in your house? Haunted is a relative term these days."

"I don't spray my plasma all over the place." I shake my head. "Excuse me, but I'm a little more than freaked out. You think it was Chloe?" I ask Logan.

"No." Barron answers for him. "It was more than likely one of the Fem minions doing the bidding of the Counts, I gather."

"Why would they bother?"

"Why would they bother?" He parrots, amused at my line of questioning. "They would bother my dear"—he pauses to pick up the results from the blood sample— "because you happen to be a rare and wanted species. Your levels came in as pure."

"How can I be pure if my mother's not a Celestra?"

He shakes his head. "It's impossible. Your mother must be a Celestra for you to be a pure breed."

I swallow nervously. I don't know which I dislike more, the fact I'm being compared as though I were a horse, or the fact my mother is indeed a Celestra and finds the need to hide it from me even after I grilled her.

"Pure." Logan appears bewildered by the news. He looks at his uncle sternly, and they share a few brief moments worth of solemn expressions.

"It's not good news is it?" I think the answer is obvious. In a perfect world there would be more Celestras, and the Counts wouldn't feel threatened.

"Normally it wouldn't be good news Skyla, but Logan tells me you have my mother's pendant. Wear it. It's the only one of its kind."

"The *only* one?" Panic shifts in slow boiling circles just beneath my chest.

"It's been passed down from the ancients—the heroes of old, the men of renown." He presses into a polite smile. "It needs to be gifted to you for it to work. And Logan here generously gifted it to you at his own expense."

I gulp down a dry pocket of air.

"I'm very thankful." Mournful, is more like it. I'd love to blame Logan for not highlighting the finer points of Celestra 101, but it's my fault for not heeding his warning to begin with. If I knew he was going to be right all of the time, I would have taken him much more seriously.

"So now that you have the pendant I don't feel too bad sharing this last bit of unexpected news." He breaks out in a genuine smile.

"What?" Logan leans in impatient.

"The blood sample has been stolen. There was a break in at the lab—after I ran the tests of course. It doesn't surprise me. Those Fem's can smell Nephilim blood from thousands of miles away. Put them on the right scent and it's not a challenge anymore."

"What do you mean, put them on the right scent?" I think I know, but I want to hear it from him.

"It means someone directed them to you first, then they went hunting for your blood. They probably found it in minutes. Decimated the lab."

"That means they're already after her," Logan says.

"They will be until she dons the pendant." He turns back to me. "And after that too, waiting for it to disappear from your neck. Oh, they would have a field day with you. You're young and beautiful. They might even try to breed you with their kind to empower their gene pools."

"Breed me? I'm not some animal you can lock up in a cage and force to have a litter of babies."

"You are if they catch you. It's a part of the price of being pure."

A part of me wants to ask if by pure he means virgin. Because if my virginity ups my value in any way then by all means I'll do whatever it takes to save my life. But I know better.

"Put that pendant on as soon as you get home." Logan is stern and direct with me.

He chose my safety over his, just like he chose Chloe's before me, and I've gone and ruined it. I'll be dead soon just like Chloe.

I'll tell my mother. She'll hire a bodyguard for me. I'll pull the money out of my college fund, only I don't have one, and Tad would never agree to that.

Face it. I'm a dead girl walking.

46

Change

Turns out Mia and Melissa can't keep a secret.

Tad and my mother have 'somehow' been apprised of the fact Logan was in my room and that I disappeared with him for several hours.

Since their initial tirade, they've been hitting websites like e-realestate.com pretty hard with various parts of the country on display—as in moving. They're in a total frenzy trying to find permanent placement before school starts in two weeks. Tad's already talking about an all girls boarding school for me. Not that it would matter much without Logan.

It's worse than death knowing I'll be away from him. I'd rather be eaten by a thousand rotting Fem's than leave him here in Michelle's eager clutches.

I watch as the fog billows out the window in silent abundant bursts. The trees stand stoic in its wake, like dark foot soldiers at the ready, just waiting for a command. I don't think we've seen the sun but twice the entire time we've been here. The thought of moving to some cheerful sunny location depresses the hell out of me. I like the moody, grey days. I like the cool of the fog on my skin, how you can inhale the day, swallow it down and make it become a part of you.

I see Brielle waving me over from her balcony so I head over without explanation to Tad or my mother. It's not that I'm making a point to be rude, it's just that I've sworn an oath to myself to never speak to either one of them again. And if they move, I won't speak at all. There's a comfort in my silence. It might be the one thing in my life I'll ever be able to control. They can try to shake my vocal cords out of me if they want, but I'm not using them. I'll be known as the mute girl forever more.

"Hey!" Brielle's face contorts with panic. "What's wrong?" She takes my head on her shoulder, pats it softly from behind.

"They're going to move," I hum into her shoulder. Her shirt smells faintly of bleach and a nice brand of softener my mother used to buy pre-Tad. It's a frivolous expense I heard him once tell her. I wish she would let him know he was too, of the emotional variety.

"Who's going to move?" Brielle sounds distressed as we take a seat on the dirty wicker bench.

"We are." I thumb back at the house. "Can I move in with you?" I ask hopeful, knowing full well my parents wouldn't allow it. I doubt at this point I could even spend the night, which reminds me, I should bring her a copy of the legal document they drew up on my behalf. I bet her mother would choke on her soy latte if she laid eyes on it. She might even spring for a lawyer in an effort to help me get legally emancipated from such barbaric circumstances.

"Yes. That would be a blast. And for sure my mom wouldn't care about whatever has them miffed. Don't your sisters love it here? And what about Drake? You can't take Drake." She spreads her hand in front of her in a mild panic. I watch mesmerized as her long pale fingers melt into the fog. I've never noticed before what pretty fingernails she has. Mine are so brittle they never make it past my skin.

"My sisters hate the house. They think it's haunted. And Drake's a moron. Nobody listens to him." True and true. I take the blame for my sisters, but I stand by what I said about Drake. At the end of the day though, he's not half bad, plus Brielle likes him and I like Brielle.

"Oh ho-ney!" She rubs my back over and over until her mother comes out to join us.

Brielle fills her in on the situation.

"Well you just got here. They need to give the place a shot. Its no wonder they think you're acting out. You're just trying to piece together this new life they gave you. I bet no one asked your opinion when they left L.A."

Actually they did, but now that I think back, when they asked *if I was all for the move* it was probably just a rhetorical question.

"Natalie's having an end of summer party. Her parents have a beach house on the coast and she does this big bonfire every year. You'll have to come. I'll take you at gunpoint if I have to." Brielle gives a small laugh.

"Gunpoint?" I muse. "It might be the only way."

I call Logan with the devastating news. He doesn't say anything for a real long time, and it makes me wonder if he's still on the other line.

"It's my fault," he offers.

"No trust me. Everything is my fault these days."

"I can't believe this." He blows out a breath. "I can visit."

"I doubt they'll let you."

"We'll apply to the same universities."

"And if we don't get in the same ones?"

"Paragon has an awesome community college."

I perk up a little. We make a depressing round of small talk before hanging up. It's probably better that I'm away from Paragon. I'm a walking time bomb. I reach over and snatch Chloe's diary off my nightstand. I pull it in close to my chest and let it warm against my body.

I swore to her I'd never read it. I'm not really afraid of Chloe haunting me or even showing up in my dreams anymore. It's like we're old friends. I don't think I'd mind it.

I roll around on my bed as sleep eludes me.

Wish I had that pendant. Wish I could give it back to Logan—keep it at the same time.

Wish it were Tad instead of me that this nebulous enemy was trying to kill.

47

Spree

Brielle's mom, Darla, has become the new go-between for me and my parents. She somehow gets them to let me have a sleepover with Bree tonight *and* attend Natalie's party tomorrow. Clearly, she could sell snow to an Eskimo and sand to an Arab. The only concession being, that she would be present the entire time. It's not her fault she forgot she had a date with her boyfriend. But she trusts us. It's nice to be treated like an adult by somebody.

"What exactly does your mom do?" I ask fanning my nails back and forth over my head. I convinced Brielle we should both have black fingernails for tomorrow in expression of our deep, deep mourning over me leaving. I actually heard mom say she was glad she didn't unpack the last of the boxes and how much she didn't look forward to starting the process all over again.

"She works in real estate. She wasn't the one who sold your parents the house, but she was amazed they bought it sight unseen."

"Tad's stupid that way," I say chipping off a dried bit of paint from off the fleshy part of my thumb.

"You really think they're going to send you to an all girl's school?" Brielle would probably have some sort of hormonal meltdown if she had to do that. It would be like sequestering the fox from the chicken coop.

"If it costs money, no. Tad can squeeze pennies from his ass. And he won't spend a single one of them on me." I pull my knees up and smooth out my long white nightdress. "I found Chloe's secret room." I wondered why she hadn't told me about it herself, but I figured maybe it was too painful, too many memories, or that it was *their* space.

"Are the butterflies still there?" She stops fanning her nails midair.

"All of them."

A steady set of heavy footsteps rises slowly up the stairs.

Brielle and I head into panic mode and sit up, each in our own corner of the bed.

"Who's there?" She shouts.

I break free from my paralysis and slam the door shut before they have a chance to answer.

"There's no lock!" Her voice shrills out to nothing.

I pan the area, but there's no dresser, not one thing of great heft that could keep someone out. A pair of black oversized scissors garners my attention. I leap over to the desk and arm myself.

A slow methodical knock, rasps against the door.

Brielle lets out a bloodcurdling scream before ducking under her pillow.

My heart thumps unnaturally, like a thousand wild horses trampling through my bloodstream. I try to steady my breathing, try to ignore the thought of mom and my sisters mourning me at my funeral—Logan—his disappointment in me when he realizes I don't have the pendant. All I know for sure is I'm going to kill the beast on the other side of the door. I'm going to start stabbing and not stop. I'm going to show the Counts that I'm willing to fight. I'll fight harder than Chloe, if she even fought at all. I'll make it impossible for them to keep me for two weeks alive. And I promise on my father's grave, no one is going to breed me like a dog in a kennel.

The door swings open and a tall man in a trench coat stands erect and threatening less than a foot away. Screaming at the top of my lungs, I plant the first puncture deep in his flesh right above his stomach—dead center.

He doubles over and lets out a yell as he falls to his knees. I jab wildly at his back, but I can't penetrate his leather coat. Before I can go for his eyes, Darla shows up and binds my wrist with her hands, while joining me in a series of wild primitive screams.

"Shut up! Shut up!" I hear her shout. "Darrell!" She rolls him over and he lets out a groan before passing out. She looks right at me. "Call 911. I think you just killed my boyfriend."

Tad and Mom sit stunned across from me at the kitchen table.

The police officers actually commended me for defending myself so well. Since we weren't expecting anyone, naturally we thought he was an intruder. Of course I thought I knew he was a Fem hired out to kill me for my pure angelic blood, but I don't share any of that information because it sounds ludicrous, and the psych ward at Paragon Hospital isn't exactly where I want to sleep tonight, or any night ever.

"Were the two of you drinking?" Tad asks rather morbidly.

"No. I don't drink."

"Smoking weed?" He continues with his exceptionally calm inquisition.

"I don't do that either. And no we weren't doing anything, but our nails." I hold up my black smudged fingertips trying to ignore the fact I probably still have blood encrusted in them.

"If he decides to press charges, this could go on your record." My mother is in a genuine state of panic.

"He's not going to. The officer I talked to said it was self-defense, and I won't get in trouble. Besides, they said it probably wasn't more than a flesh wound."

Tad shakes his head. "It's like you've become this huge liability overnight. Did it ever occur to you to ask who it was?"

"We did." I think Tad's the liability.

My cell goes off, and it's a text from Logan.

I've long suspected you were lethal.

I slip my phone back under my thigh. I don't feel like ticking off Tad or my mother anymore by texting while they try to break me.

"We think you need counseling, Skyla." My mother measures her words. Her cheeks have hollowed out since we've been here, and she has dark circles under her eyes the size of half dollars.

"We met with a local therapist a few days ago." Tad interjects. "It was just a consult. We never imagined you were capable of something like this, but now I'm afraid we're going to have to insist."

"I don't have any problem going to a therapist." If he's on Paragon, they'll have to stay.

"I'm really glad you feel that way." Tad gives a sad smile. "We called him a few minutes ago. He thinks we should bring you in for a full evaluation this evening."

"It's two in the morning. What kind of doctor works at this hour?" I ask. Something doesn't smell right.

"Actually," my mom says with tears in her eyes. "He wants you to check into the hospital so you can have a goodnights rest when he's ready to see you." Her lips twitch. Her lips always twitch when she stretches the truth.

"Are you taking me to the psych ward?" Words I never thought would come from my lips.

"Yes."

48

Spooked

Paragon hospital lies smack in the center of the island. The fog has rolled back into the sea, and I see the bare naked landscape under the harsh disclosure of a sharp white moon.

Tad confiscated my cell phone before we left the house. I wasn't allowed to say bye to the girls because they were sleeping. Drake came out looking sleep deprived, and when they told him where they were taking me and why, his face bleached out.

The doctor will probably discover things about me I never knew—that I'm a killer and lock me up forever. I really believe that somehow I killed Chloe. Even if I wasn't responsible for the destruction of her life, I hastened it just like Logan implied.

We pull into a tall rectangle of a building. A glossy white brick path leads into a set of double sliding doors, and a blast of warm air hits me. I hadn't even realized I was cold.

The elevator goes up for days, spits us out onto violent red carpet and a reception area with a nurse out front. A set of double wood doors with tiny, boxed shaped windows is the only other thing around.

A male nurse in bright blue scrubs emerges from inside. He holds the door open and extends his hand for us to enter.

I'm part way inside before I notice my mother and Tad aren't trailing. Tad is already pushing the button for the next set of elevators, and my mother gives a silent wave as the nurse shuts the door behind him.

They weren't going to come inside. No long, drawn out goodbye, no kiss from my mother—just a half hearted wave goodbye—the cold slam of the door.

Tears fill the crook of my arm. I lay on a glorified elongated box that's bolted into the floor with no sheets and no pillow, locked in a dark room by myself.

"Skyla." A familiar voice originates from the side.

I jump back and scream. There's a small ray of light beaming in from the nurses station.

"It's me, Gage."

I rush into his arms and collapse in a fit of heaving sobs.

"I can't stay." He whispers into my hair. "They'll check you every fifteen minutes. Logan wants you to go to sleep. He can visit you there."

"He can? Why didn't he tell me?"

"He was saving it." He tightens his grip on me. "They're coming. Goodnight." He presses his lips against my forehead until he disappears.

I use the back of my arm as a tissue and wipe a long streak of snot across the entire length of it. I still haven't showered. I can feel the sticky residue of blood in places I missed, high up near my elbows, the crevices of my wrist. Lying back down, I start to drift into beautiful dreams that will soon be filled with Logan.

Logan dreams us near a crystal blue lake on a bright summer day, in some other place far from Paragon where the sun isn't afraid to shine.

We wrap our arms around each other on a grassy knoll so steep we're almost vertical.

"Comfortable?" He asks wiping the tears from my eyes.

"Yes." My voice sounds muffled, and I wonder if it has anything to do with me being locked in a padded room.

"You're going to be fine."

"Did Gage say so? Why didn't I think of that? I should have made Gage tell me everything about my future."

"It's not right of him to do that." Logan strokes my hair. It calms me down. Makes me want to stay in this dream forever.

"I'm desperate," I say.

"You don't need to be. Take in the Master's peace. He wants this anxiety, give it to Him."

"I don't know how to send it."

He lies back on the emerald lawn. A deflated balloon appears on his fingertips.

"What's that?"

"Your anti-stress agent. Imagine all of your stress filling up this balloon. Come on." He urges.

I imagine all of the anxiety, the fear, the hurt, rejection, loneliness—*grief*, filling up that balloon.

In one fell swoop it bloats the size of a basketball. Logan ties it off on the bottom and simply lets go.

"There it goes." He says mock shooting it with his fingers.

We watch as it reduces in size, as it turns into a speck and blinks out of existence. The celestial blue of the sky is increasingly deeper near the northern portion—stars are visible—right here midday.

"It's done." I feel lighter from the effort. "Thanks."

"Don't thank me."

"Right. *Thanks*," I call up to the sky.

There's so much more I don't understand. So many more balloons to fill in this lifetime. I wonder how He has time to hear them all or if they accumulate around Him until He's overwhelmed. I imagine I'll get to ask Him myself one day. He'll show me a pile of decimated latex, and I'll get to thank Him all over.

We fall asleep safe in one another's arms. Logan and I intertwined. I don't think I'll ever sleep alone again.

49

Out

Breakfast is served in the dayroom with a group of individuals who are either stoned or genuine zombies.

A nurse, with a severe case of adult acne, supervises with a clipboard, circling the table in a rotational manner that actually makes me dizzy.

All of the windows are barricaded with either wood framing or some kind of metal bars that make long rectangular patterns alternating with shorter squares, and some of those are in color.

Along the back wall, a giant piece of butcher paper is taped up behind the television. It's a picture of a cabin by a lake with a boat bobbing in the middle, all done in magic marker, and it reeks of third grade. This is what my life has come to, breakfast with zombies and finger-paints.

A short woman dressed in an over cheery shade of pink, slaps a plastic tray with a covered dome in front of me. I pull the lid off ready for the big reveal, hopeful for something palatable even though I'm not that hungry. It's a small bowl of white foamy mush, a piece of burnt toast, and a small portion of lumpy scrambled eggs that smell like a wet dog. I replace the dome and sink down in my seat.

Without asking, the rather over eager zombie to my left glides my tray over and grunts into it. He quickly dumps my portions into his own tray and slides mine back empty.

Great. Guess I'll wait for the next fresh serving of brains.

"Skyla Messenger?" A slim man with dark hair and thick-framed glasses leans into the dayroom clutching at my chart. "Come with me, please."

I follow behind him a good two feet, down the never-ending hall. I can feel the air rising up through my pale yellow gown, my sticky-back socks catching on the carpet all the way over.

He unlocks an over-bright room equipped with two seats and a table, asks me to be seated before clicking the door shut behind us.

"Dr. Booth." His face brightens. He's got tiny brown eyes shadowed by furry brows, and he's just now starting to remind me a little of a teddy bear. He flops the chart on the table and folds his arm high up on his chest, examining me.

"Am I supposed to say something?"

He shakes his head rather bored. It's like the door shut and he's loosened. He probably does this with all his patients. He's nothing more than a big fake that bilks insurance companies. He'll probably want to keep me locked up for the next five years to insure his annual Hawaiian vacation.

"I want to go home," I say weak.

"I'm going to let you, but first we need to have a little talk."

A surge of adrenaline percolates through me. He's going to let me go home!

"Yes, anything." I'll make stuff up, tell him whatever he wants to hear, just get me out of here.

"I know who you are, Skyla. I know you're a Celestra."

Oh God. Oh no. He's one of them. Tad sent me right into the arms of some psycho Count who wants to kill me. He's probably going to keep me locked up for good, and issue a battery of blood tests until I have none left.

"I'm Levatio." He gives a tiny laugh and offers his hand.

"Really?" I shake his hand. "One of my good friends is Levatio!" I'm surging now. I've beat Tad at his own game.

"Gage Oliver," he says knowing. "I've known the Oliver's from times and times past." He widens his ultra calm smile.

"So you're going to let me go, right?" Maybe he can convince my parent's I'm totally sane, lock Tad up instead.

"I'll let you go, but I might have to incarcerate you from time to time just to make it look good." He stretches his smile then snaps it back to the way it was.

"What?"

"Kidding." He pats me on the arm before leaning deep into his seat. "I know the problems you Celestra have. You're the one client I'll have to pay special attention to. Logan mentioned you have a hedge pendant?"

"*Did.* I sent it back in time." It sounds insane even to say it. "Please don't tell. I want to be the one to tell him."

"Barron mentioned that your blood was stolen from the lab. It means the Countenance has access to your full genetic code. They're going to want to stop you from ever having children if they don't kill you first. But that's not a worry for today. And they've certainly let other Celestra live. If they were to wipe out the entire race it might ignite a civil conflict." His forehead creases dramatically and a look of genuine worry crosses his face.

"How many are left?"

"I don't know, but the numbers aren't impressive."

"Please, just send me home." I pick off the polish on my fingernails. It's a nervous habit, and since I'm prone to being nervous I don't usually wear nail polish to begin with.

"I'll have the nurse return your things. I've already called your parents. They'll be here momentarily. I've told them I'd wave my office fees since your insurance doesn't cover all of it. Your stepfather was so thrilled he mentioned it might be worth hanging around."

"As in not move?" I don't believe this. It's too good to be true.

"Here's my number." He slides over a card. "If you need anything, and I mean anything, I'm more than willing to help you. My great grandmother was a Celestra." He nods with pride.

"And what happened to her?"

"She married a full blood Levatio, so they left her alone."

He leads me back out into the hall, shakes my hand, and tells me I'll see him as minimally as possible.

I change into my clothes, and the nurse unlocks the door. My mother is alone at the end of the hallway by the window. I go over to her, and we watch the rain on the other side of the glass together in silence.

"Skyla." She pulls me into a big weepy hug. "Will you ever forgive me?"

"Of course." I feel lighter than air being outside of those double locked doors.

It's Tad I won't forgive.

50

Escape

The girls still believe I spent the night at Brielle's. No one told them otherwise so they were none the wiser. Drake, on the other hand, invites me to his room in an effort to pick my brain for hours.

"Did they strap you to the bed? That's standard protocol." He adds as though he were preempting my answer.

"No. They put me in a room with a bed and no pillow. I had to sleep in a gown."

"A gown?" He asks incredulously. "You could have hung yourself with a gown."

"Yeah, well I didn't. I don't think there was anyplace to hang myself from." Not that I'd use that as a means of transportation to the nether world. It's disgusting. And according to years of lingering in the back of a church—heavily frowned upon.

"Did they force feed you meds?" He's gripped. With a father like Tad he might find out firsthand how it all plays out in there.

"They didn't give me any."

"No meds?" His brows narrow dramatically.

Obviously I've let him down with this bit of information.

"No, they just took turns beating me with a stick. Then the other patients tried to eat my brain for breakfast. That's where they keep the real zombies, you know."

Drake has gone from the world's biggest enthusiast to completely unamused.

"I'd love to sit and chat, but I've got a party to go to."

"Natalie's party?" I push back on his bed a notch. It's on the beach, which I've never seen because Paragon seems to be locked in a fog tunnel. "I want to go."

"You *are* nuts. You're never going anywhere again." He plucks a t-shirt from out of his dresser.

"But it's the end of summer."

"It'll be the end of your life if you go." He pulls out a pair of jeans from his closet. "I gotta change."

I roll my legs off the bed, landing on the cool of the hardwood floors.

I'm not going miss the biggest party of the summer. I may only have months to live. Besides, what's the worse that can happen if I go?

It turns out Tad has another notarized copy of the one I destroyed. I don't hesitate signing the agreement this time, just before everyone sails off to bed. It's not like I'm going to do any of those things anyway, and sneaking out of the house is not listed so I won't be breaking code. Plus if it gets him off my back I'd sign ten of them.

In the butterfly room I press against the walls until I hit a seam of cold air and push. A small doorway opens, and I'm in the attic. I hold out my cell phone for light, and tread along the planked pathway until I hit the window facing Brielle's house. I can't remember what's outside the window. I lift the glass and am more than impressed to find a small landing that leads to a lower roofline that leads to the porch. They all look doable this way, but I'm not so sure about coming back. Then again Logan did it. Never mind the fact Logan just so happens to have the strength of a hundred Sumo wrestlers.

Brielle and Drake are already in her Jeep. Drake looks terrified as though my lawless behavior might rub off and cost him a night in the psych ward, too.

We take the coastal route. It's magical at night with the moon spraying its light across the water. I can't wait to take a nice relaxing walk with Logan, feel the sand between my toes. We can skip rocks and cuddle by the fire, roast marshmallows on the open flame.

"I have the very distinct feeling of foreboding," Drake announces in a dramatic fashion from the back.

"So like, you want me to pull over so you can puke?" Brielle contorts her features with utter disgust.

"No, *foreboding*," he repeats. "It means eminent danger, misfortune up ahead. I've felt like this before and bad things happened. I've got this sixth sense for danger."

"So I'll drive slow. And I won't drink. Arrive alive." Her voice ends on an up note.

The possibilities of Drake's premonition jag in my brain like an out of control train. How come I don't feel any of these things? Shouldn't I be the one with some built in warning system?

The radio goes to static, and Brielle leans in and switches it off.

A car stalled on the side of the road garners our attention. The hazards are blinking and there's a woman scissoring her hands wildly into the air.

"Looks like she needs help." Brielle doesn't hesitate to pull in behind her.

"Are you nuts?" I ask. "She could have a gun or be an ax murderer. It's eleven thirty at night. We don't need to be helping anybody."

"Relax. She probably just needs to borrow my cell or something. It's not L.A., sheesh." Brielle gets out and walks over. The woman steps into the beams from Brielle's headlights. There's something familiar about the woman's wild frizzy mane. Brielle pulls her cell out of her pocket and hands it over.

"Look's like she was right," I say looking back at Drake.

A pair of headlights slow and pull in behind the Jeep.

"Looks like help has arrived for the helpers." Drake leans back and closes his eyes.

I watch as a large framed man comes over to the driver's side window.

Brielle is so right. I would have had ten thousand panic attacks by now if this was L.A., but it's Paragon. Paragon, where you could probably walk the streets alone, barefoot and naked, and still nothing would happen to you.

The woman standing with Brielle walks up toward the front of the car. She looks right at me and starts in on a spasmodic wave.

A scream gets locked in my throat. It's her! The woman, the ghost—the whatever who hung herself outside my kitchen door!

I start in on a spasm of wild panting and pointing.

"What?" Drake leans into the front seat.

A man jumps out of the shadows and snatches Brielle, stuffing her into the backseat of the car.

Without warning the woman jumps into the driver's seat of Brielle's car, and a man appears next to Drake.

I don't think the back door ever opened.

I don't think either of them are human.

51

Taken

We drive for miles through the backwoods of Paragon. Drake is bound and gagged, and both our cells have been confiscated. The guy in the backseat who happens to be wearing a black ski mask has managed to secure my hands behind my back with plastic ties and placed a blinder over my eyes.

After a long, severely bumpy ride, the car crawls to a stop, and the driver's door opens. The night air is heavily scented and reminds me of an Italian seasoning my mother uses that I absolutely hate.

The bandana gets ripped off my head and part of my hair with it.

"Ouch." I see the woman's car from the side of the road just up ahead, so that must mean Brielle's here too. I look around for signs of either Bree or Drake, but it's eerily quiet. They've both mysteriously disappeared.

"Come on." The masked man plucks me from the car. He pulls at me to follow, but I'm stuck. My hands are catching on the seatbelt. When he strapped the makeshift handcuffs on me, he didn't realize my belt was still on.

"Get her hands out." The woman hisses.

Her face is an odd shade of grey and her hands are skin over bone with long knobby fingers that look twice the size they need to be.

"I can't, it's stuck and these things are a bitch to get off. I need a knife."

"Then get a knife!" She shrills into the night air eliciting a series of echoes.

He reaches into the ground and opens a small door. I watch in amazement as the hole in the earth lights up, and he descends down a stairwell.

It's some kind of underground passage. Who's ever going to find me down there?

The lone baritone chirp from a high up branch adjacent to where I'm standing captures my attention.

It's the raven! I remember how Logan put his finger to his mouth and pointed toward the east, and the bird took off and sent Gage over—only my hands are bound. I doubt I'll be able to do the same thing. I swear it's looking at me—watching.

Go and get Gage. I think right at the bird. It's Gage's bird, I surmise. It's always a precursor to when I see him. If Logan had a cool bird like that, I'm sure he would have told me. Actually I take that back. Apparently he's not above saving tricks for later.

Go and get Gage! I shout as hard as I can in my mind. Still nothing.

I can almost hear Logan telling me gifts can be learned. Right now I want to learn to talk to birds. I hear Logan whisper the word *believe* into my subconscious. OK. I shut my eyes tight. *I believe you will get Gage for me now.* I look up, still nothing.

It's funny, but I do believe this. I do believe the bird is going to get Gage, and I'm going to get out of this mess, and everything's going to be just fine.

Just then the bird takes off and a swell of relief fills my chest.

I let go of a huge breath I didn't even realize I was holding and give a hint of a smile.

A giant man in a ski mask comes right at me.

"No." I shake my head.

He holds up a machete and grunts as he slices the seat belt right off my shoulder from the back.

All of the relief I felt a moment ago has drained. I let out a scream as he picks me up and carries me below the surface of the earth.

Long, winding corridors—spacious corridors at that. It's well lit, painted stark white with matching glossy floors. It reminds me a little of West Paragon High, and I have a gut feeling Logan and I aren't going to have any classes together down here either.

"Can you let my friends go?" I don't dare call Drake my brother. They'd drag him off to the chop shop if I even implied it.

"Shut up. I hate the sound of your voice," the woman snaps. Her flame-red shaggy hair billows out as her voice continues to echo.

"What's wrong with my voice?" Actually I didn't mean to say that out loud, I was more—

"Silence," her caustic screech ricochets off the walls.

I hate *your* voice I want to tell her.

"You're going to love it here." She motions to a stark white room with a large stainless tray that strikingly resembles the one Logan showed me at the morgue.

Shit! I wiggle like mad to free myself from the strong mans grip.

The woman opens a tiny door in the back and I fall in like a sack of potatoes. I look back to see her waving before shutting the door. A small glass window shows them moving around, sliding a tray on casters with an assortment of sharp tools toward the metal bed. The guy with the mask pours a dark red liquid inside it and starts scrubbing it down.

"They're sanitizing it," a male voice whispers from behind.

"Gage!" I cling to him so tight I think I'm going to push through.

"Logan's on his way."

"Can't you just zap me out of here? I'll believe it and everything," I sputter the words in a desperate panic.

"It doesn't work like that." He reaches over to the plastic ties binding my hands and I feel a release of pressure. He holds up a set of tiny pliers before slipping them back into his pocket.

"So you can never be contained? No one can ever trap a Levatio?" That's the first gift I'm going to learn.

"Not true. All they have to do is touch me and I can be bound."

The door behind me rattles. I can see her red fiery hair rising in the window. My arms fall loose to my sides as Gage blinks out of the room.

"We're ready," she sings.

52

Tinder

"Let go of me!" I shriek as the masked man drags me over to the table. "No!" I yell. He places his hand over my mouth and I bite down hard.

"Hey!" He barks plucking his finger from my teeth.

While he inspects his wounds I take the opportunity to lift my knee aggressively into his crotch. He lets out a slow moan, moving to the side like an injured puppy. I don't see scary lady with the freaky bad hair, so I bolt out of the room and start running down the hallway.

What if I was supposed to go left, and I went right? I come upon a series of shut doors, and I'm too afraid to open them. I can't help Brielle or Drake. I'm a lousy angel. And who asked me if I wanted this, anyway? Soon as I get out of here I'm going to get a blood transfusion. I want out—out of this crazy hamster maze, away from bat-shit crazy people who want to kill me. I never asked to be a Celestra. I never wanted this. If I didn't come to Paragon and meet Logan I'd still be living my clueless life back in L.A. where I'd be shopping and hitting the beach and probably getting killed trying to navigate a twisted L.A. freeway...like my father.

I stop running. I'm not sure, but I think I made a revolution around the place— only the door to the slaughter house is now closed. It's no use. They're probably watching me on their security cameras, or using their sixth sense, while I wear myself out.

Gage where are you? I shout into my mind with all my might.

God, help me.

A slight buzz erupts just beneath my feet.

Huh?

It happens again. It's not an earthquake. I'm familiar with those. This is right underneath my shoes. I take a step forward and it happens again, but stronger. I start walking and it picks up, but when I go to make a left down the hall it stops.

Should I follow the buzzing? Are buzzing feet good or bad? Good vibrations. Is that what this is?

Gage? I continue to follow the buzz. If I'm going to get sliced and diced, I may as well get a free foot massage out of it.

The vibrations increase. They file through my leg and up my torso, rattling my bones. It's probably some slow form of electrocution, and I'm too hopped up on adrenalin to notice. The vibrations expand into deep sweltering waves. They ride up my body until I start to feel a familiar rhythm in my brain, something...I can't put my finger on it. I've done this before.

I clasp the side of the hall, lean into it and feel the cool of the wall against my cheek. Feels like I'm falling asleep on my feet, like I'm tumbling through the air in a freefall.

The radio goes to static, and Brielle leans in and switches it off.

A car stalled on the side of the road garners our attention. The hazards are blinking and there's a woman scissoring her hands wildly into the air.

"I'm back," I pant in disbelief.

"Looks like she needs help." Brielle starts to pull in behind her.

"No! You have to drive. Trust me on this," I scream, navigating the car back out onto the street. "She could have a gun or be an ax murderer. It's eleven thirty at night. We don't need to be helping anybody." I scramble for my phone to call Logan.

"Relax. She probably just needs to borrow my cell or something. It's not L.A., sheesh." Brielle tries to pull over again.

"You can't do this!" I shout. "She's going to kidnap you. I saw the whole thing. You were right Drake, something very bad was about to happen." My chest heaves in and out in a dramatic fashion. I'm sure I'm making no sense to them, but I just got released from the psych ward, and I haven't spent my insanity allowance yet.

"OK, relax. I know you can't wait to see Logan. I'll get you there. Besides, look." She points into the rearview mirror. "There's another car already helping. See? It's not L.A." She picks up speed and continues down the road.

Not L.A. that's for damn sure.

Logan, smart boy he is, greets me with a luxuriously long mouthwatering kiss. My toes dig into the cool sand below as the heavy smoke-filled scent of the bonfire swirls around us.

He pulls back and relaxes his hands around my neck. His eyes glitter as they focus in on mine with great ferocity.

"You are not going to believe what just happened." Truthfully I don't even want to talk about it. The words sort of flew out of my mouth without permission.

"Skyla, I know." His fingers sink into my shoulders. "What you're experiencing is called a Treble. It means this reality is temporary, and things will be changed back to the way they were before you left."

"No!" My body begins in on a series of involuntary quivers. "Drake and Brielle are there, and I don't know where they are." A rise of panic starts ripping through me as my teeth start to chatter.

"Tell me something about where you are so I can find it."

"I'm underground. It's...we drove along a bumpy road, and there was a forest." I close my eyes. I've just described all of Paragon. "Don't you have some underground detection kit or something? It's a facility. It has a steel table like the one from the morgue. Do something!" I'm shaking uncontrollably. "Call the police." My arms vacillate before me, transparent as velum. "Don't let me go Logan. I don't want to die."

Logan's eyes ignite with frustration.

Then he does a wonderful thing. He kisses me—a hungry kiss that quells my shivering body. He pushes his tongue into the back of my throat deeper and deeper, increasing his grasp on me until I think he's going to thrust right through me and my pleasure is mixed with pain. Before I can push him away, I disappear.

53

Back

It takes a few hard blinks for the blinding white walls to come into focus. I let out a moan of defeat when I realize where I am.

"Come on." Someone grabs my hand from behind and tugs.

"Logan!" I throw myself on him despite the fact he's already moving, and we start dashing down the hall. "We can't just leave. Drake and Brielle are here, too."

"I'm sensing." He pats his hands up and down a series of doors.

"Over here," Gage hisses from around the corner.

"Gage," I yell, as Logan and I move toward him.

A white metal door pulsates from the inside.

"Bree? Drake?" I shout through the crack. "We'll get you out."

"Back up." Logan holds his hand out. His fingers twist the knob with such sheer force he creates an impression of his hand in the metal. The door slides open then bounces wide as Brielle and Drake burst through.

"I know the way." Drake leads us down the twisted corridor and points to a shaft in the ceiling. "That's it." He pants, staring at the square ten feet above us.

Gage starts wobbling on his feet. He starts in on a slow gravity-defeating rise to the top of the ceiling.

"What the?" Drake's voice is less than a whisper. His face loses all color and he drops to his feet in a disheveled lump on the floor.

Logan lifts him up and hands him to Gage, then Bree.

"Thank you," a voice echoes around us.

"It's her." I can feel her nearby.

"Get them out of here." Logan directs Gage.

A swarm of bodies dressed in black crowd in on Logan and me. One of the men pinches the back of Logan's neck and he falls, limp as a rag doll.

"Logan!" I'm tossed over the shoulders of an exceptionally tall man and dragged right back to the chop shop.

I'm bound and strapped with metal chains thick as my thumb, lying on the glorified stainless bathtub of death.

"This really sucks," I say rather calm as the redheaded woman works in a frenzy, separating long glass tubes into rows and rows. "So what's your name?" I ask trembling.

"Whatever you'd like to call me." Her voice echoes without reason. She doesn't bother turning around from her busy work.

"I'll call you, Hateful. You can't have any good in you to do something like this."

"I prefer Ezrina. And what is it you think I'm doing?" She sorts through a box before plucking out more enormous vials.

"Getting ready to take my blood."

"One point for you," she says it dry as though she were wasting her time speaking.

"I can't stand the sight of blood." My chest heaves in huge waves of panic.

"Then I'll gouge out your eyes first." She clicks a few vials together clearing out her workspace.

"No. No thanks." I struggle to pull my hands free from the chains.

"Relax, will you?" She sits on a stool and glides over like I'm about to have a physical. "You Celestras are always so edgy."

I stare wide-eyed behind her at Gage, holding a metal like spear in his hand.

The sharp end of the blade ejects itself out of her chest. She looks down at it in disbelief as a pool of crimson blooms across her white shirt like a flower.

She falls over and begins to twitch and writhe. A series of gagging noises sputter from her as I watch in horror from above. She points at me, her eyes narrow in with intense hatred, then blood trickles out of her nose and she stops moving.

My feet loosen. Gage is twisting metal, plucking my legs free. He makes his way over to my arms and starts doing the same.

"You killed her!" I never thought I'd be so elated over witnessing something so gruesome. "You were fantastic."

"Yeah well, she doesn't stay dead, so let's hurry."

"What do you mean she doesn't stay dead?" I ask, rubbing at my wrist.

"We have two hours." He helps me up. "I'll go get Logan." He disappears.

A short stubby man dressed in black, slides sideways through the door. He races over and I back into a tray of medieval looking tools of the trade.

I grab the first thing available—a long twisted piece of metal with a spear like tip. My thumb glides over a bump near the bottom, and the thing starts spinning.

"OK, hand it over and no one gets hurt." He laughs without meaning to.

With everything in me, I thrust it hard into the soft fleshy area just below his stomach. He tumbles backward thrashing and screaming. I grab the metal tray and run behind him, knocking him over the head with it.

"Nice work," Logan marvels, as he and Gage come upon me.

We three stand over his body as the blood spills out in a small pool around his midsection.

"How long does he stay dead?" I ask.

"Forever," Gage comments.

I look from Gage to Logan.

"I thought you said it was a two hour thing?"

"Not this one." Gage pats his jeans. "Let's go."

We race down the hall at top speed. Logan helps me out through the overhead panel and back onto the forest floor.

We follow Gage through the thicket in the woods and find Drake and Brielle huddled down below the windows in the backseat of her Jeep.

"I let them in on your little secret." Gage climbs into the backseat with them.

Logan helps me get in on the passenger's side then hops around and starts the car.

It's going to be a long ride home.

54

Safe

Logan helps me up to the butterfly room. Without him I probably would have never been able to crest that second roofline.

I take off my jacket and toss it down the open panel onto my closet floor.

"So how does it feel being an angel?" He asks sitting across from me clasping my hands.

"Exhausting. It won't always be like this will it?"

"It might be if you don't put on that pendant."

Color rises to my cheeks, as I stare down at our interlocked hands.

I'm sorry. I don't have it anymore. I accidentally gave it back to Chloe.

A soft sigh depresses from his chest. He looks to the side before blinking back to me.

It's not your fault, Skyla. I should have been upfront with you right from the beginning instead of leaking information to you on a need to know basis.

"Should we go back and get it?"

"You've returned it," he gazes past my shoulder, "it may not help you now. Besides, now that she knows we're after it, Chloe will want to secure it."

"Do you forgive me?" It comes out meek.

"There's nothing to forgive. Skyla, I want to tell you everything." He gives a gentle tug. "Chloe was a Celestra too."

"Really?" I like her more just because of that. I sort of have this sisterly vibe going with her.

"Really," he pauses, "I had to break it off with her, but she didn't want to."

"What do you mean had to?"

"Two Celestra make a very big bull's eye."

"Oh." I don't think I like where this is going.

"Two Celestra dating, are too stupid to live," he continues.

"Excuse me?"

"You and I, we can't see each other anymore," he takes in a breath, "not publicly."

"So we'll date in private." I don't really like it, but I'll take what I can get.

"It's not that simple. We need to take it a step further."

I don't want to know what that could possibly mean.

"You need to have a boyfriend. A real person who everyone thinks—believes you're with."

"Who in their right mind is going to agree to that?"

"Gage," he closes his eyes as he says his name.

"Gage," I repeat. "His prediction—it's probably a fake marriage."

"Let's hope." He twists his lips.

"So when does this start?"

"I think it should take effect now. And trust me, Gage made it clear that he would make this very believable."

A flashback of Lexy Bakova's party flickers through my mind—Gage and I locked in a kiss.

"I know," he says mournfully.

"I'm so sorry."

"Don't be. I was stupid to let Michelle hang all over me."

"What about you? Are you going to get a girlfriend?"

"Nope. I'm going to be the scary loner." His chest rumbles with a dry laugh.

"What would we have to do to be together permanently?"

"Take down the Countenance." He shakes his head as though this were impossible.

I crawl over and sit between his knees. He drapes his arms around me, and I lean up and kiss him gently on the lips. "Then that's what we'll do."

Thank you for reading **Ethereal (Celestra Series Book 1)**. If you enjoyed this book please consider leaving a review at your point of purchase.

*The following is a preview of Celestra's companion series, **EPHEMERAL (The Countenance Trilogy 1)**.

Ephemeral

The Countenance Trilogy 1
Preview

Addison Moore

http://addisonmoorewrites.blogspot.com/

Copyright © 2012 by Addison Moore

Preface

I used to believe in things, in people, in places, and names—concrete forms of life that ended at some point in the unknowable future. I used to believe memories were infallible, that they could never collapse around you like a house of cards, burn to cinders before ever touching the ground.

People vanish all the time. Other people. You hear about it on the news, see their smiling faces staring back at you on milk cartons—their pictures plastered around town like wanted posters. But it was a world within a world, and innately you knew this could never really happen.

I used to believe in death. I used to believe once they put you in that box and tucked you away for one very long night under six feet of soil it was finished. The sunlight, fresh air, a warm embrace, they would never be yours again. It was the final vanishing act—your curtain pulled down and covering your casket. That was the day it would all start anew. Staring into the face of God, awaiting your final judgment.

But I was wrong about everything.

I had my name, my life, and my eternal judgment revoked in one passing hour at the hands of madmen who share my bloodlines.

They took everything, but my memory. They tried and failed, and now I am nothing more than a liability—a spark in a bed of dried timber, waiting to unleash an inferno. I don't know how long I can go before they stop me or if they even care.

I used to believe so easily and now I strain the most insignificant detail from each passing day as if it were poison.

I know one solid truth. Everything about this new world is a lie.

I'm going to infiltrate their ranks—dismantle their kingdom—take them down until they all vanish, evaporate like smoke from the planet, erase any memory of them as if they had never happened.

Or I'll die trying.

And I just might.

1

In Memory of Me

In the grand scheme of things, you'll be dead for a lot longer than you'll ever be alive.

I marinate in that truth, baste in the beauty of its wisdom while peering out at the dull emerald world. I fumble through dense woods with roots that race throughout the forest floor like wild petrified snakes. Wisps of lamp-lit fog twist throughout the narrow trails as gnarled branches coil around the evergreens.

Something stirs from behind, disrupts the silence with the heavy crush of leaves. I jump—startled, as though waking from a very bad dream. My chest thumps in rhythm to the pounding in my head.

"Hello?" I call out.

I try to remember how I got here. The last solid memory I have is driving to my boyfriend Tucker's house to rip him a new one for sleeping with Megan Bartlett, a girl I know from volleyball. I was distracted with rage, the light turned green, and I never saw the other car coming. Then the crash—I remember kissing the windshield as I bristled through it at a horrific velocity.

A groan emits from the branches—more rattling.

My feet crush over a bed of dried maple leaves, filling in the haunting void of silence.

A hard thud lands square behind me, and I turn slow on my heels.

It would have been understandable to see a deer, a bear, or even another human being. But this...

A whimper gets caught in my throat, drowns out the idea of a scream.

It's a man—a thing, his grey skin decomposed beyond recognition, exposing dried muscle and bone over his forehead, one eye missing, teeth all but gone. It staggers forward, slashing the air with a violent swing.

Before I can start in on a full-blown sprint, I trip over an errant branch and land hard on my back.

It comes at me—falls on its knees beside me omitting a sharp putrid stench. Crooked fingers tear my sweater, easy as shredding paper.

I let out a gurgled cry, twist and claw, scampering to my feet.

The forest gyrates, turns into a viridian kaleidoscope as I fumble through a dizzy maze of branches.

Loud guttural moans vibrate throughout the woods. I can feel its footsteps seconds behind. The forest darkens, the fog presses against the branches, fills my nostrils with its oily haze.

This is a nightmare—this is hell—a nightmare with a trapdoor. None of this is real. It can't be.

My breathing quickens, my head starts to spin as I navigate the spindles in the thicket.

My mother once said, most people are prone to run through this world blind. I remember her words, the soft mannerism in which she spoke them as I stumble from branch to branch—rip a hole in my jeans, lose my jacket on the offshoot of a pine.

The creature gains speed, touches me. Grazes over my hair with its necrotic fingertips. I race blindly through the woods, push past the searing pain ripping through my skull, and crash to the ground with finality.

I glance back, fully expecting to find the decaying body, the stench of death, but instead I find a boy my age—the look of surprise ripe on his face. He pulls me to safety behind the trunk of a tree and lunges at the creature. He plucks a knife from his back pocket and wrestles the beast as it tries to latch onto his face.

I pick up a loose branch near my feet and give a hard jab at the monster, striking it right in the groin. It gives a soft gurgle as if laughing at my efforts.

I pick a rock up off the ground, the size of football, and lob it at the tangle of flesh rolling around in front of me.

It hits the boy in the side of the head, and he lets out an agonizing groan.

Shit!

"Sorry," I shout.

He flips the creature, and lands it hard on its back. Its face holds a lavender hue, blue lips, unnatural bumps and lesions over the cheek and partially decomposed forehead.

It looks as if the boy is pummeling its malformed face, but as I approach from the side I can see him digging the knife into the creature's eye, over and over until it ceases to writhe beneath him.

He jumps up and cleans his blade against the soft trunk of a maple.

The creature sizzles. Its ragged clothes engulf in flames quick as a grassfire before extinguishing itself in a ball of smoke.

"What's happening?" I pant.

"Don't you know?" He replaces the knife in his back pocket. The hard line of his jaw pops as he suppresses a smile. "They're biodegradable," a rumble of laughter trembles out of him. "You OK?" He comes over and cradles the side of my face with his open palm, observing me as though he were a doctor. A stream of light falls over him, amplifies the fact he's alarmingly handsome.

I want to say, I don't know where the hell I am, but I think there are more pressing matters than my lack of topographical orientation.

"What was that?" I ask.

His brows knit together. He leans in to inspect me, skeptical that I even had to ask.

"What's your name?" He asks, wiping the dirt off his jeans.

"Laken Stewart." I place my hand over the warmth of his arm. "Where am I?" I've never been twenty miles from where I was born—hell I've never left Kansas. For sure, I've never seen a forest this dense, let alone drifted in one.

"Ephemeral," he dips into me with his gaze, "Connecticut," he adds with a touch of sarcasm.

"I think I'm lost." I touch my fingers to my temple as an explosion of pain rips through me.

Laken.

In the distance a woman shouts my name.

"Looks like you've just been found." He offers a reserved smile, holds my gaze a little longer than necessary before turning away.

There's something intoxicating about this stranger, this earthly savior of mine, and a part of me wants to discover everything about him.

"Wait." I catch him by the elbow. "What was that thing?"

He doesn't say a word, just gazes at me perplexed and sorrowful.

"Laken?" The female voice spikes with agitation.

"I'd better go," he takes a full step back, "nice meeting you."

"You saved me," I say. He disappears in the fog like an apparition. "Hey—what's your name?" I shout after him, but he doesn't answer.

"Laken!" A raven-haired woman dressed in a power suit and heels snatches me by the wrist. "You need to keep out of the woods. Do you understand?" Her hair is slicked back in a knot, reflecting blue shadows as she moves.

"Who are you?" I pull my hand back.

"It's me, Laken—Ms. Paxton," she offers a short-lived smile. "You need to get back to campus." Her chest rises violently as she struggles to catch her breath. "Never venture outside of the academy."

She guides me out of the oppressive forest onto a red brick path that rolls out toward a monolithic series of ivy-covered buildings.

"Your uncle requested that you meet up with your brother tonight."

"My brother?" Fletcher died well over a year ago, along with Wes, the only boy I ever loved. They drank their way into oblivion before taking one last fatal swim in the lake.

"Yes," it strangles out of her, "do you think this is funny?"

"No." I rub my bare arms. "I'm confused, I—"

She shoves a yellow student card at me. "You dropped this on your little jaunt in the woods."

Laken Anderson—right face, wrong name. Issue date September 4th. Junior, Ephemeral Academy.

"Ephemeral." I test the word out on my tongue. I stare at the student card, confused as hell as to what it might mean.

"You're a resident at Austen House." Her lips twist with pride as if she procured the living quarters for me herself. "I realize how overwhelming your first day must be. Your sister's the dorm mother. She's been waiting to orient you all afternoon."

"My sister?" I have two, Jen is studying abroad her second year of college, and the epicenter of Lacey's world is plundering all my free time to help plan for her epic tenth birthday party. I love Lacey. I couldn't love her more if I had her myself.

"Jen—your sister, Jen." Ms. Paxton nods in frustration. Her eyes widen with horror as she circles over me with an epiphany. "I have to go." She darts down the road in the opposite direction.

"Wait!" I call out as she evaporates into the evening shadows.

I don't have a brother anymore.

I don't have an uncle.

My mother is a drunk, and my sister Jen left the country first chance she got. I live in Cider Plains, Kansas, in a quickly dilapidating bungalow that belonged to my grandmother, which is safely haunted by her pissed off ghost and the curse she bestowed upon us before she hung herself from the rafters.

My last name is Stewart, not Anderson. After I shot through the windshield, a tall radiant being declared it was not my time. He placed his hand, the size of a catcher's mitt, over my face and submerged me back onto the planet.

I know for a fact I died on July 13th the day before my cheating boyfriend's seventeenth birthday. Two calendar months have dissolved without my knowledge. Here I am—same body, different name.

All I really want to know is what the hell is going on.

Acknowledgements

Thank you to my wonderful family for putting up with mountains of laundry and lots of questionable nutrition. And to my husband who finds the time to do things that help me in every way even when he's dog-tired. I love you guys.

To my awesome readers who have found a heart for Celestra, you amaze me.

To the Master who sits on the throne, I owe you everything.

About the Author

Addison Moore is a *New York Times, USA Today,* and *Wall Street Journal* bestselling author who writes contemporary and paranormal romance. Her work has been featured in *Cosmopolitan* Magazine. Previously she worked as a therapist on a locked psychiatric unit for nearly a decade. She resides on the West Coast with her husband, four wonderful children, and two dogs where she eats too much chocolate and stays up way too late. When she's not writing, she's reading. Addison's Celestra Series has been optioned for film by 20th Century Fox.

Feel free to visit her at:

http://addisonmoorewrites.blogspot.com
Facebook: Addison Moore Author
Twitter: @AddisonMoore
Instagram: @authorAddisonMoore

Made in the USA
San Bernardino, CA
18 November 2016